A Ghost Of Christmas Past

Also by Anthony M. Strong

JOHN DECKER THRILLER SERIES

What Vengeance Comes

Cold Sanctuary

Crimson Deep

Grendel's Labyrinth

Whitechapel Rising

Black Tide

Ghost Canyon

Cryptid Quest

Last Resort

Dark Force

A Ghost of Christmas Past

Deadly Crossing

Final Destiny

JOHN DECKER SERIES PREQUEL

Soul Catcher

THE REMNANTS SERIES

The Remnants of Yesterday

The Silence of Tomorrow

STANDALONE BOOKS AND NOVELLAS

The Haunting of Willow House

Crow Song

WRITING AS A.M. STRONG

Mystery Crime Thrillers

THE PATTERSON BLAKE SERIES

Never Lie to Me

Sister Where Are You

Is She Really Gone

All The Dead Girls

A Ghost Of Christmas Past

A John Decker Holiday Novella

Anthony M. Strong

WEST
STREET

West Street Publishing

Cover art and interior design by Bad Dog Media, LLC.

ISBN: 978-1-942207-41-2

To my readers everywhere...
Happy Holidays!

One

JOHN DECKER WANDERED Bond Street while the snow fell in a wintry haze. It was late morning the day before Christmas Eve in the year 1911, a Saturday, and Decker had never felt so far from home. Excited shoppers milled around in a holiday-fueled frenzy buying up every last item on display in the windows of the exclusive department stores and specialty purveyors that lined the famous London street. But Decker was not there to shop. He merely wanted to escape the lonely suite of rooms provided for him by the Order of St. George after his arrival in Edwardian England.

Decker had led a solitary existence in the weeks since finding himself stranded in early twentieth-century London, especially since his friend and fellow time-traveler Mina had been abducted in the small town of Mavendale by persons unknown. Her disappearance, coupled with his longing to get back to Nancy, who he would have married if fate had not intervened and thrust him over a hundred years into the past, had left Decker something of a hermit outside of work.

Decker paused in front of a jeweler's window that displayed a dazzling selection of cut gemstones set in rings and necklaces that far exceeded the craftsmanship of any jewelry store he had ever shopped in. The prices, even in 1911, reflected this. He wished he could buy Nancy a gift, even if it never reached her. But as he looked at the glittering wares on display behind the jeweler's window, Decker realized this was not what he wanted to choose if it was destined to be the last gift he ever bought her. A gift that she may never see. The jewelry was beautiful but not personal. He wanted to find something that would surprise and delight her.

He continued on, strolling down the street to kill time and provide a distraction from his melancholy thoughts. The Christmas season only heightened this sense of isolation. He would have done anything to see Nancy's smiling face or taste her homemade eggnog as she prepared the Christmas meal while humming carols to which she barely knew the words.

Decker continued, weaving through the holiday crowds browsing the high-end shops for last-minute gifts. He passed by high-end clothing stores displaying Saville Row suits and women's dresses from the continent. There was a shop that sold hats of all shapes and sizes. Perfect for a day in the country or a trip to the races.

And then he saw it tucked between a men's tailor and a pharmacy.

Sedgwick's Book Sellers of Bond Street.

Decker stopped and looked at the volumes on offer in the window. There was a central display surrounding a miniature Christmas tree and, underneath it, titles that he recognized as classics but which were new in the first decade of the 20th century. The Secret Garden. Peter Pan. The Wizard of Oz.

Next to these, in a separate display, was a more mature book —the Lair of the White Worm by Bram Stoker.

Decker felt a lump rise in his throat. Nancy loved to read and would have cherished owning any of these antique books, which of course, were nothing of the sort at this moment in time.

Unable to resist, Decker entered the shop. A bell sounded as the door closed behind him. A small man with spectacles appeared from a dark room behind the counter at the far side of the store.

"Welcome. Is there anything specific I can help you find, sir?"

"I'm just browsing," replied Decker, wiping snowflakes off his coat.

"Very well. If you need assistance, I shall be at your service."

Decker thanked the man and stepped between the aisles, browsing the shelves loaded with volumes. The bookshop was laden with a pleasant scent of paper and ink that hung in the air. It brought Decker back to his childhood, browsing the used bookstore in Wolf Haven, searching for novels of adventure and intrigue. Once, when they were dating before he left for the police academy and New York, he had taken Nancy into the bookstore, and she had pulled novels from the shelves and talked excitedly about each with wide eyes. She had an eclectic taste ranging from the classics to modern genre fiction, and he had always admired her ability to get lost in a good book. The question was what he should buy a woman that was separated in time by more than a century. Then he saw it sitting on the shelf among a collection of titles he did not recognize.

A Christmas Carol by Charles Dickens.

Decker pulled the thin book out from among its peers on the shelf. It was bound in plain red cloth with the name and author embossed on the front cover and spine. He opened it and flicked through the pages to find them in excellent condition, apart from a bit of foxing around the edges. But this was not surprising given the age of the book, which was printed in 1843 according to the front matter. It was then that Decker realized he was holding a first edition.

It was too much to resist.

He approached the counter and placed it down. "How much do you want for this?" He asked.

The shopkeeper rubbed his chin. "That's a rare book you have there. I wasn't even aware we had it."

"How much?"

The shopkeeper shrugged. "How about two quid."

Two pounds. Decker did some quick arithmetic in his head. That amounted to about two hundred and fifty dollars in twenty-first-century terms. A bargain, considering. He smiled and reached into his pocket, placing a pair of pound notes on the counter. "Consider it done."

"Thank you kindly, sir." The shopkeeper made short work of stuffing the money into his cash register. "Would you like me to wrap it?"

"Sure." Decker waited for the shopkeeper to package the volume in brown paper tied with string before taking it and heading back out onto the street. As he left, the bell above the door tinkled again. He allowed himself a moment of satisfaction for the first time since arriving in London. He had a wonderful gift for Nancy. The only question was, how on earth would he get it to her across the ages?

Two

DECKER TOOK a hansom cab back to his suite of rooms near Hyde Park. By the time they pulled up at the three-story building, light sleet was falling. He climbed out and paid the driver, giving him a larger-than-usual tip because it was Christmas, then hurried inside with his collar tipped against the chill and the book in one hand.

Decker's rooms were on the second floor. He climbed the stairs and let himself in, then shucked off his coat and hung it on a hook before heading to the formal sitting room and placing the book on the shelf. He put a log in the grate along with newspaper and kindling and was reaching for a match to light it when there was a knock at the door.

Thomas Finch, his boss and head of the Order of St. George, was standing on the other side.

"Decker, my good man. Merry Christmas," he said in a voice rather too cheery for Decker's mood.

"I was thinking of skipping the holidays this year," Decker replied, motioning for him to come in.

Finch hesitated a moment as if summing up Decker's state-

5

ment, then he stepped across the threshold and brushed light flakes of snow from his collar. "Looks like we are in for a white Christmas."

"I can't say I'm all that keen on snow," Decker replied. "Christmas or otherwise."

"You're in a fine mood."

Decker shrugged.

"What are you planning to do? Mope around your rooms for the season with a long face?"

"That sounds just fine to me," Decker said. "It's not like I have much to celebrate under the circumstances."

"Just as I thought." Finch walked into the sitting room and looked around. "You don't even have a tree."

Decker shrugged again. "Did you just come here to harass me, or do you have some valid business?"

"Funny you should say that, but I do have a reason to be here, although it is anything but business. I was afraid you would find no joy in the holiday season, so I arranged for you to accompany my family and me to our Christmas gathering outside the city."

"No, thank you."

"I thought you would say that, too, but I'm not taking no for an answer. Pack a bag and be quick about it. Our transportation is waiting."

"I already told you; I don't wish to accompany you for some holiday gathering in the country. Take your cheer elsewhere."

"Goodness. If I didn't know better, I'd say you had turned into Ebenezer Scrooge."

Decker couldn't help but smile despite himself. An hour ago, he had picked up a copy of A Christmas Carol, which he intended to give to Nancy when and if he ever saw her again. Now Thomas Finch was likening him to the main protagonist in that same book. He heard Nancy's voice ringing in his head, telling him not to be such a grouch and make the most of it. "Scrooge, huh?"

"Just a little." Finch paused. "Come on, man. Some Christmas spirit will do you good."

"Now *you* sound like the Ghost of Christmas Present," Decker quipped.

"Funny. Will you accompany me to the country willingly, or do I have to call my man up here to drag you out?"

"Fine. I'll come along to your Christmas shindig."

"My Christmas what?"

"Never mind. What's the deal with this gathering, anyway?"

"Our good friends, Lord Percy and Lady Elizabeth Goodridge-Smythe, have recently purchased a country manor in the Home Counties and are eager to fill it with laughter this Christmas. To that end, they have invited a small group of friends to celebrate with them. Since you are all alone, I asked them if I might bring you along. They were happy to oblige, especially when I told them you are American."

"I'm not sure what my nationality has to do with anything," Decker grumbled.

"Lady Elizabeth spent some time in the States before she was married. Boston, I believe. I'm sure she will be eager to reminisce."

"Ah. For a minute, I thought you were implying I would be the entertainment."

"I'm sure there will be plenty of entertainment without resorting to your sardonic wit. The Goodridge-Smythes' have something of a reputation for throwing interesting parties. Their New Year's Eve ball of 1905 is still talked about in grand parlors across the city."

"I've already said yes. You can ease off the sales pitch."

"I was merely saying that it will not be a dull affair." Finch pushed his hands into his pockets. "Now, I don't wish to hurry you, but Lily and Daisy are waiting, and I would rather not delay us any longer than necessary."

"Daisy?" Decker had never met Finch's daughter. "I thought she was away at boarding school?"

"She is, but naturally, we bring her home over the Christmas holiday. Now, if you could hurry, dear boy."

"Give me five minutes." Decker went to the bedroom and grabbed a tweed travel bag, which he packed with sufficient clothes for three days. Maybe Finch was right. He had been acting like a Scrooge. Decker closed the bag and buckled it, then returned to the sitting room. "I'm ready."

"Excellent." Finch started toward the front door. "I promise you a splendid time."

"I shall hold you to that," Decker said, putting his coat on and following Finch.

They made their way downstairs and stepped outside. A black horse-drawn carriage was waiting at the curb.

Decker looked at it, surprised. "No motorcar today?"

"I thought we would take a more appropriate form of transportation, especially given that the weather is due to worsen."

"Fine with me," Decker said.

The coachman climbed down and took his bag, stowing it in the trunk at the rear of the carriage.

Finch opened the door and allowed Decker to climb in before joining him.

Lily smiled when Decker sat on the seat opposite her. "It's a pleasure to meet you again, Mr. Decker."

"Likewise," Decker replied.

Sitting next to Finch's wife was a seventeen-year-old girl with cascading blonde hair and fine features.

"This is our daughter, Daisy," Finch said, settling next to Decker.

The young woman smiled. "Hello."

Decker returned the smile. "Hello. I've heard a lot about you from your father."

"Nothing too dreadful, I hope?" Daisy's smile vanished, but there was a twinkle of mischief in her eyes.

"Not at all," Decker said. "Just the opposite."

"In that case, he shall remain in my good books."

"How magnanimous of you," Finch said to her. He picked up a walking stick leaning against the seat and tapped it twice on the window above their head. "Driver, whenever you're ready."

"Aye, sir," came the reply. Then the carriage jerked forward, and they were on their way.

Three

TWO HOURS AFTER LEAVING LONDON, they arrived at the grand house in the country, surrounded by rolling fields and farmland as far as the eye could see. The sleet had turned to snow, covering the landscape in a white blanket that made the going more treacherous. Along the way, Lily made small talk, deftly avoiding any mention of her husband's work or Decker's situation. She fell silent as they pulled through the wrought-iron gates leading up to the house and peered out the carriage window.

The driveway was long, perhaps a mile, and wound through what must have been lush formal gardens when it was not concealed by snow. As they approached the main house, Decker noticed a smaller building standing a few hundred feet away. It was constructed of sandstone with Gothic arched windows squared off with spandrels and inset with fine stained glass. A square tower graced one end.

"That must be the chapel," Finch said, craning his neck to see past his wife. "Percy said there was one on the grounds, but I didn't imagine it would be so grand. I must say, this estate is rather more lavish than I had imagined."

"You sound positively jealous," Lily said, a slight smile touching her lips.

"Not in the least, my dear." Finch shook his head. "I have neither the money nor the inclination to maintain such an imposing property. Percy is welcome to it, although I have no problem being entertained here over the holidays. It makes a pleasant change from the city."

"What do you think, Mr. Decker?" Daisy asked. "Are you overawed by the grandeur of your surroundings?"

"I think it's very nice," Decker said, looking up at the manor house as their carriage pulled around in front of it. "But a little too large to be practical."

"Well said," Finch agreed, opening the door and stepping down onto the driveway. He turned and helped Lily and Daisy out of the carriage.

Decker was the last to disembark. He looked up at the house. The house was built of the same sandstone as the chapel. Tall rectangular leaded windows looked out under steeply pitched roof lines. Turrets stood at both ends. An ornate porte-cochère framed the main entrance.

No sooner had they alighted from the carriage than the front door opened to reveal a middle-aged woman with a short-cropped bob haircut dressed in a matching brown skirt and blouse.

"Thomas, you made it," she said, greeting them at the door, then turning her attention to Decker. "This must be the American you told me about."

"That would be me," Decker replied, introducing himself.

"I'm lady Elizabeth Goodridge-Smythe. But my friends call me Lizzie." She motioned for them to enter. "Please, come inside out of the elements. I would hate for my guests to catch a chill when they've only just arrived."

"Thank you." Decker followed Lady Elizabeth inside and found himself in an expansive grand entrance hall with a sweeping dark oak staircase.

To his left was a library. Shelves stuffed with books rose from floor to ceiling. On the right, through an open door, he saw a dining room. A table with enough seating for at least twenty people was set for dinner with fine silverware, cut crystal glass, and a large festive centerpiece of a stag's head in silver surrounded by a wreath of Holly and Ivy. The air was redolent with the scent of pine mixed with a faint aroma that reminded Decker of the holiday meals his mother had cooked when he was a child.

An enormous cut crystal chandelier hung in the center of the entrance hall, its flickering gas mantles twinkling like a thousand fireflies and lighting the space in a soft, warm glow.

Portraits hung on the walls of the entrance hall. Somber renditions of stern-looking men and delicate featured women who stared out from their canvasses as if they were annoyed to be dead.

Lady Elizabeth noticed Decker's interest in the paintings. "Those were here when we bought the manor. Fifteen generations of the Blackthorn family." She pointed to one painting near the library door of a couple in their sixties dressed in Elizabethan garments. It looked old. Much older than most of the others. "Those are Edmund and Phillipa Blackthorn. Edmund built the manor back in the sixteenth century."

"They look serious," Decker said.

"No doubt," Lady Elizabeth replied. "They lived in troubled times." She turned her attention from the painting. "But enough of the history lesson. It's Christmas. We have more pleasant things to do."

Decker nodded. "We do, indeed."

The coachman was bringing the bags inside. He set them on the floor. After ensuring everyone was settled, he climbed back into the carriage and moved off toward the stables. A butler dressed in a black morning suit and white gloves stepped forward and closed the front door just as footsteps rang on the tiled floor.

Decker glanced around to see a lean middle-aged gentleman with dark hair and piercing blue eyes emerge from the room next to the library. He approached them with a jovial grin on his face. "Thomas, you're here!" he exclaimed, greeting Finch with a hearty slap to the back. "And, of course, your lovely family."

"This is my husband, Percy," Elizabeth said to Decker.

"And you must be the gentleman Thomas told us about," Percy said, turning to Decker and extending a hand in greeting. "I'm so pleased you could make it. Elizabeth has a wonderful evening planned."

"Which I'm all too eager to hear about," Finch said, turning his attention to Elizabeth. "Your gatherings are never dull, Lizzie."

"I should hope not." Elizabeth laughed. "But my lips are sealed. You will have to wait until after dinner to discover what I have planned. But first, you must settle in."

"We shall convene in the drawing room at seven," Percy said. "The other guests are already here and eager to meet you all, no doubt."

"I can hardly wait." Finch turned his attention to Elizabeth. "Perhaps you will give us a clue regarding the evening's entertainment."

"Not a chance. I shall resist all attempts to extract even the smallest hint." Elizabeth smiled demurely and clapped her hands. As if by magic, a pair of maids appeared. She turned to them. "Please show our guests to their rooms so they may freshen up."

"And then we'll get the party started," said Percy enthusiastically. "After all, it's Christmas!"

Four

THE BEDROOM DECKER found himself in looked more like a high-end hotel room, he thought, than a room in someone's house. It was at least four times as big as his bedroom back in London. An enormous four-poster bed with silk drapes tied back at the posts dominated the space. The floor was oak planks dinged with character, over which was laid a finely woven Persian rug in a floral motif. Even the furniture was grand, with an intricately carved wardrobe and bureau sitting on opposite walls. A carved walnut library armchair upholstered in a pattern that complemented the rug sat in one corner.

Decker placed his bag on the bed and changed from his travel clothes into more formal attire. That done, he left the room and went back downstairs, where he was directed to the door behind the library from which Percy had emerged earlier. It turned out to be a drawing room with dark oak paneling cladding the walls and a gorgeous, coffered ceiling. A pair of camelback sofas stood opposite each other in the center of the room. Intricately rendered oil paintings of classical English landscapes hung on the walls. A tall Christmas tree festooned with ornaments stood in front of the window, underneath which presents of all shapes and sizes had been placed. Decker recognized several that had been in the trunk of the carriage that had brought them here and regretted not having any presents of his own to place under the tree.

A fire burned in a great stone hearth that provided a focal point for the room. Several of the other male guests had already congregated there and were gathered around Percy, who was regaling them with a humorous anecdote about his work in the city.

Decker noticed Thomas Finch standing with a glass of brandy and joined him.

"Mr. Decker, allow me to introduce everyone," Percy said, turning his attention to the pair after finishing his story. He went around the group, which, apart from Finch, comprised a rotund city banker named William Fitzmorris, a lanky politician named Edward Lark, and a portly businessman named Archibald Stour. All three were middle-aged. When the introductions were done, Percy glanced toward Finch. "I was about to ask Thomas how the pair of you became acquainted."

"John is a colleague of mine," Finch replied casually. "He's on loan from our cousins in The States as an advisor."

"Ah. This mysterious government department that you refuse to talk about," Percy said with a laugh. "If I didn't know better, I would assume you are engaged in some kind of subterfuge, given how little you talk about your work. I sit in the Lords, and even I know nothing about your department except that it raids the government coffers on a regular basis."

"You make us sound like thieves," Finch replied.

"Not at all, my dear boy. But it would be nice to know what our money is going toward."

"Trust me, Percy, those that need to know already do." Finch shot Decker a quick warning glance not to elaborate further regarding their work, which Percy appeared to believe was nothing more than an obscure department within the British Government.

Decker had no intention of discussing the Order of St. George. He accepted a brandy in a tulip-shaped glass from the butler, who was flitting around the room making sure everyone had what they needed.

"Always playing close to your chest," Percy said with a chuckle. "I can appreciate that."

The butler disappeared, carrying the empty silver tray that previously held brandy glasses, then reappeared a few minutes later and stood in the drawing room doorway. "Gentlemen, if you would like to make your way to the dining room, dinner will be served shortly."

They headed toward the dining room, drinks in hand. When they entered, the lady of the house, Elizabeth, was waiting along with three other women, including Lily. Also present were Finch's daughter, Daisy, and two children—a boy of about ten and a girl of around eight years old—that Decker had not previously seen.

The pleasant aroma of food hung in the air.

Elizabeth stepped forward and took the lead, introducing everyone for a second time. The older of the two women was Florence, married to Edward Lark, the politician. The children were obviously theirs, judging by how they clung close to the woman. The younger woman, slender and attractive, was married to the banker, Fitzmorris.

Decker said hello to each woman in turn and politely took their hands. Afterward, the group took their seats, and the meal was served.

Five

FIRST CAME a rich and creamy mushroom soup, which everyone present devoured in near silence. As the maids cleaned the bowls away to prepare for the main course, the banker, Fitzmorris, cleared his throat and took a long swig of brandy before addressing Percy, who sat at one end of the long table opposite his wife who had taken a position at the other. "I must say, this is an absolutely fabulous house you have here," he said, with a trace of envy in his voice.

"Thank you, William," Percy replied. "It has also turned into something of a money pit."

"But well worth every penny," Elizabeth said. She turned to Decker, who was sitting to her right next to Finch and his family. "We purchased Blackthorn Manor in the spring from an old acquaintance of Percy's in the Lords who was looking to retire and liquidate some of his assets. Alistair Blackthorn. This was his ancestral seat. The estate has been in his family since it was built. He even sold us the furniture and fixtures, such as they were. The manor was in a dreadful state, and we spent most of the summer

17

restoring the place and replacing rotten furniture before it was in livable condition."

"We even had to fix the roof," Percy grumbled. "Darned thing was leaking like a sieve. I would never have taken it on if I had known just how much the building had fallen into disrepair."

"Yes, you would," Elizabeth said. "You love being the Lord of the Manor. And one could hardly grumble at the price. We got it for a song. Even with all the money put into the renovations, we would still turn a handsome profit should we decide to sell."

"Really?" said the banker. "You must have got yourselves a hell of a deal. I'm surprised anyone would agree to sell such a grand house for so little."

"Probably has something to do with the fact that Alistair loathes the place," Percy said. "It makes me wonder what he knows that I don't. Not that he would ever tell me."

"There's a straightforward explanation, my dear," Elizabeth said. "It's the ghost."

A ripple of nervous anticipation ran through the guests at the table. Eden, the banker's wife, who was at least ten years younger than her husband and attractive enough that she had possibly married for money, let out a slight squeal.

"Do you mean to say that we're staying in a real haunted house?" She asked with wide eyes.

"If the stories are true, then Blackthorn Manor is indeed haunted." Elizabeth took a sip of wine.

"You're saying a spirit drove off the previous owners?" The politician, Edward Lark, gave a derisive snort. "I don't believe in ghosts."

"Maybe you will after spending Christmas at Blackthorn Manor, Edward."

"I wouldn't count your chickens," replied the unflappable politician.

"Have you seen a ghost yourselves?" Eden asked.

"I'm afraid not. We have only spent a few weeks here since we renovated the house. Percy's grueling schedule in London makes it hard to get away. Although..."

"Yes?" Eden leaned forward.

"You *have* seen something, haven't you," said Lark's wife, Florence. Apparently, she did not share her husband's disbelief. "Do tell."

"It really isn't very interesting. As I said, I did not see a ghost. But one dark and dreary evening last month, when Percy had gone back to London overnight for business, I was sitting in the drawing room in front of a warming fire reading one of my favorite books when I felt an eldritch presence right alongside me. The room grew colder, and I thought the fire had gone out. But when I looked up, it was still burning brightly."

"Ooh, how spooky." Florence shuddered and leaned close to the table. "What happened next?"

"I sat there, stiff as a board and afraid to move. Davies, the Butler, had already retired for the night, as had the maids, so I was utterly alone. The lights flickered once, twice, then a third time. The room had become so cold that I could see my breath in the air. Then, the sensation slipped away as quickly as it had come."

"An overactive imagination. That's all it was," Percy said from the other end of the table. "Brought about by too much digging into the history of the house."

"What about the history of the house?" Lily asked, enraptured.

"It's a silly story, nothing more." Percy shook his head. "I haven't found a shred of evidence to support its validity."

"What story?" Eden sounded practically beside herself with curiosity. "You can't mention such a thing and then not tell us."

"I agree," said Lily.

"It's really not as exciting as one might imagine." Elizabeth finished her wine and waited while it was refilled, then continued. "This house was built in the sixteenth century and, as such, has its share of stories, including a phantom priest dressed in a black cassock and even a ghostly horse in the stables, but the one to which I attribute my strange encounter dates back a hundred years. The Blackthorns in residence at the time had two daughters and a son. The girls were older. Nine and thirteen. The boy was barely seven years old. It was the night before Christmas, and they were tucked up in bed, eagerly awaiting the arrival of a certain red-suited gentleman in his sleigh.

"The boy, it is said, could not contain his curiosity and crept downstairs in the early hours to search for Father Christmas and the toys he would bring. The sisters heard his small footsteps in the corridor and peeked out of their bedroom door but saw nobody there. They were unsure what to do but eventually decided to return to their beds, afraid their parents would catch them wandering the house when they should be asleep. The next morning, the boy was discovered missing, and the girls told their parents what they had heard. The house was searched from top to bottom, and the constable called from town. For a week, they searched to no avail. They even scoured the woods and fields around the house, but of the boy, there was no sign. The boy's mother died of a broken heart shortly after, and his father turned to drink."

"They never found the boy?" Eden asked.

"To this day, no one knows what happened to that young boy in the early hours of Christmas morning on a frozen and snowy night much like this one."

"That's because nothing happened to him," Percy said as the main course, a pork roast with potatoes and roasted carrots, arrived. "He never existed. It's a fairy tale. A story to scare the dinner guests on a stormy evening and nothing more."

"Then how do you explain all the accounts of ghostly happenings in the house ever since?" Elizabeth asked, raising an eyebrow at her husband. "The knockings and phantom foot-steps. The whispering in the darkness when no one is there. The touch of a hand on your shoulder when you are alone."

"As I already said, a hundred years of overactive imaginations and too much fine wine. Nothing more."

"We shall see," Elizabeth said with a wry smile. She picked up her knife and fork. "Later tonight, I shall prove to each of you that the spirit world is closer than you think and maybe even close enough to touch."

"I can hardly wait." Eden clapped her hands excitedly. "Do tell us all about it. Please?"

"I shall not utter another word on the matter until after dinner, so please, stop asking." Elizabeth wagged a finger. "But you will not be disappointed, that I can promise."

Six

WHEN THE MEAL WAS OVER, the entire group including the ladies this time, retired to the drawing room. The same room that Elizabeth claimed to have had her ghostly encounter in. A fire was still raging in the hearth, quickly consuming fresh logs. The soft light from wall sconces, coupled with the leaping flames, made tall shadows dance across the walls. Outside, beyond the Christmas tree that stood in the window, the snow was falling thick and fast. It would be easy, Decker thought, for a person to imagine spirits roaming such a place.

No sooner had they entered the room than Elizabeth turned to the butler, who hovered on the periphery of the group, attentive, yet mostly invisible. "Davies, are the preparations made?"

"Yes, madam," replied the butler without a hint of emotion. "I have prepared the library just as Madame Serafina requested."

"Excellent." Lady Elizabeth clasped her hands together. "Has Madame Serafina arrived yet?"

The butler nodded. "She arrived during dinner and inspected the preparations, which were to her satisfaction. I had the kitchen provide her a hot meal, after which I showed her to the bedroom you requested to be put aside for her use."

Decker glanced at Finch.

He shrugged.

The butler continued. "Would you like me to fetch her?"

"Yes, thank you, Davies."

The butler nodded a second time and withdrew from the room without another word. He pulled the doors closed behind him and left the group huddled around the hearth, full of questions.

"I say, Lizzie, what the devil are you up to?" asked Lark.

"Patience." Lady Elizabeth approached the fireplace and turned back to the group. "All will be revealed in due course."

"You're being particularly secretive this year," Fitzmorris said.

"And with good reason." Elizabeth glanced toward the drawing room door as it opened, and Davies reappeared. Behind him was a gray-haired woman who looked to be in her late fifties or early sixties. She wore a long, flowing black dress and head-scarf. Chunky silver rings adorned three fingers on each hand, each one inset with a different semiprecious stone that glinted and flashed when she moved.

Percy, now on at least his fifth brandy, turned toward the door. "Good news. The circus has arrived."

Elizabeth shot him a withering glare before turning her attention to the newcomer. "Welcome to our humble abode, Madame Serafina."

"It is a pleasure to be here among such a distinguished gathering," said Serafina in an accent that Decker could not pinpoint but sounded vaguely Eastern European.

Decker leaned close to Finch. "What's going on?" He asked under his breath.

"Damned if I know," Finch replied.

Lady Elizabeth crossed the room and met the woman in the

flowing robes halfway. She turned back to the group. "Ladies and gentlemen, may I present Madame Serafina, the greatest spirit medium London has ever seen."

"Not just London." Madame Serafina looked from one expectant face to the next. "I have recently returned from a tour of the continent where my powers were most gratefully received. I was the talk of the town in Paris, Barcelona, and Milan, to name but a few."

"A spirit medium!" Eden's face lit up. "How very spooky."

Decker leaned close to Finch. "Did you know about this?"

Finch shook his head. "Just relax and have fun. Not everything has to be so serious."

Decker turned his attention back to Madame Serafina. She was in the center of the room now, holding court.

Lady Elizabeth stood next to her and waited for the excited chatter to die down before speaking again. "I asked Madame Serafina to come here tonight to unlock the secrets of this house and put the spirits that dwell within to rest. It is my great pleasure to announce that an hour from now, at the stroke of midnight, we will hold a séance next door in the library."

The atmosphere in the room was thick with anticipation. No one spoke. The only sound was the crackling of the fire.

After a suitably dramatic pause, Lady Elizabeth continued. "With Madame Serafina's help, we will draw back the veil between the living and the dead and allow the spirits of those who wish to communicate brief entry into this world."

Madame Serafina raised her arms in dramatic fashion and waved her hands in the air. "Now, I must go and prepare for what is to come. I shall see everyone an hour from now in the library at midnight. Unless, of course, you do not wish to know what lies in the great beyond." With that, she turned and left the room with Davies, the butler, at her heel.

For a moment, no one spoke, then Eden chirped up. "Lizzie,

you've outdone yourself this time. A séance at midnight. How utterly delightful."

"And creepy," said her husband. "But what the hell? I'm game."

Lady Elizabeth was practically beaming.

Percy stepped forward. "And now, I think it's time for the children to go to bed."

There was an audible groan from the children.

The boy pulled a face. "I want to stay up for the séance."

Florence shook her head. "Out of the question, Eric."

"Please?" This was the girl.

"Absolutely not." Lark nudged his daughter toward the door.

"Come along," Florence said, taking their hands. "It's time for bed and I don't want to hear another word about it."

"But the séance," Eric protested.

"You're too young for such things, my boy," Lark said. "It will give you nightmares."

The boy's shoulders slumped. He glanced toward the tree in the window and the wrapped packages beneath. "Can I at least open a present before I go to bed?"

"Not until Christmas morning. Bed, young man. Right now."

"This is so unfair," Eric said, but even so, he let Florence lead him from the room along with his sister.

Finch turned to Daisy. "That means you, too. Time for bed."

"You can't be serious, father?" Daisy said, folding her arms. "I'm hardly a child."

"And you're hardly a woman yet, either."

"I'm seventeen." Daisy turned to Lily. "Talk to him, mother."

"I agree with your father," Lily said. "I don't want you partaking in a séance. It isn't proper for a young lady."

"You're a lady, and I don't see you going to bed," Daisy said. She flashed a sardonic smile.

"That's enough, Daisy." Finch pointed toward the door. "Do as your mother says."

Daisy hesitated a moment, as if she were contemplating some fast retort, but then she turned to Decker with a demure tilt of her head. "Good night, Mr. Decker. I shall see you in the morning." Then she turned and left the room without looking back.

Seven

THEY FILED into the library at the stroke of midnight, even as a clock somewhere deep in the house pealed twelve solemn chimes that echoed ominously through the hallways and chambers.

A round table stood in the middle of the room, over which was draped a black cloth. Eleven chairs circled the table. A mild scent of incense hung in the air, sweet and fragile. A candelabra sat on the table holding three flickering candles. The lights were off, rendering this the only illumination apart from that spilling through the library doors.

Madame Serafina sat at the furthest point from the door, her hands clad in black gloves, spread palms down on the tablecloth. Her eyes were closed as if she were sleeping, or maybe in some ethereal trance.

"Approach the table, and take your seats," Madame Serafina requested in a voice barely above a whisper, without opening her eyes or making any other movement to acknowledge their presence.

Decker noticed place cards sitting in front of the chairs, each bearing a name in scrolling cursive. He found himself seated next to Finch, with Eden and her husband to his right.

The butler, Davies, stood in the doorway, watching the proceedings with a flat expression. At Lady Elizabeth's nod, he withdrew and pulled the library's double doors closed. The light spilling from the entrance hall beyond shrank and snuffed out, leaving the candles as the only source of illumination. Darkness pressed in on all sides around the table.

Once the group settled, Madame Serafina finally opened her eyes and lifted her head to observe them. "Welcome to the parting of the veil."

A murmur of nervous excitement rippled through the assembled guests. Eden leaned close to her husband and spoke quietly in his ear, an expectant grin on her face.

"Silence." Madame Serafina snapped the order with such authority that the titters and whispered conversations were instantly cut off. "The spirits require solemn concentration, or they will not come through."

"So sorry, won't happen again," muttered the rotund businessman, Archibald Stour, who was the only other guest, aside from Decker, not to be accompanied by a partner. He glanced around the table. "This is all rather serious, what?"

"You profess to be quiet, and yet you still blabber." Serafina turned to look at Stour. "Perhaps you would be more comfortable in the drawing room with a brandy while we conduct our business with the other side?"

"Not in the least." Stour held up his hands. "You won't hear another peep from me."

Madame Serafina observed him a moment longer, and then, satisfied he had piped down, returned her gaze frontward. "There are some rules that must be obeyed if we are to converse with the spirit realm this Christmas eve night. Once we begin, no one is to move from their chair or approach me. I shall fall into a deep, trancelike state and might speak in other voices or tongues. Do not be alarmed. This is all quite normal. Again, this is part of the process, and I should not be physically disturbed. Absolute silence must be observed at all times unless I or a spirit are addressing you. The circle must not be broken for any reason while we are connected to the spirit realm, otherwise, we risk allowing those who have passed free entry back onto our plane. Only after I close the connection, shall you be free to move from your seats. Does everyone understand?"

There was a quiet chorus of affirmative replies.

"Wonderful." Madame Serafina lifted her hands from the table. "In that case, we shall begin."

Decker waited to see what would happen next. He had read about the spiritualists of the nineteenth and early twentieth century. They were almost exclusively frauds, using cheap parlor tricks, sleight of hand, darkness, and cleverly constructed props to convince their audience that the spirits walked among them, and even communicated, often relaying exactly what the gullible attendees wanted to hear. He had no reason to believe that Madame Serafina was anything but a charlatan, collecting enormous fees to perform her act in society, drawing rooms and libraries for those unwitting enough to let her dupe them.

He glanced at Finch, who looked equally skeptical, but remained silent, no doubt to avoid another group admonishment from the spirit medium.

Madame Serafina took a deep breath. Then another. She looked around at the assembled party guests, then motioned. "Would everyone kindly link hands?"

Decker took Finch's hand on one side, and Eden's on the other. He felt a slight tremble in the woman's grip, as if she were battling a case of nerves. Madame Serafina had already convinced one in their number, at least.

When all had linked hands—except for Serafina herself, who

made no move to take the hands of those on each side of her but rather, Decker noted, placed them back on the table, palms down —the medium gave one more long breath.

Her eyelids fluttered and closed.

She tilted her head toward the ceiling.

A faint breeze whipped through the room, causing the candle flames to leap like crazy dancers.

Eden let out a small whimper. Her hand gripped Decker's tighter still.

Madame Serafina moaned. Her breathing quickened.

Someone cleared their throat on the other side of the table, but the medium appeared not to notice.

Decker glanced around, wondering what would happen next. The butler, Davies, had been in this room preparing it for the medium's arrival. He wondered exactly what that entailed.

He didn't need to wait long to find out.

Madame Serafina's moans grew louder. Her head swayed from side to side in a gentle lolling motion, eyes tightly closed.

Then, without warning, the candelabra in the center of the table moved. It slid a little sideways, paused a moment, then lifted slowly into the air and hovered six inches above the tablecloth.

A couple of guests let out startled gasps.

Another breeze, stronger this time, whipped through the room, seeming to come from somewhere behind Madame Serafina. Then, all at once, the candles blew out and deluged the library in inky blackness.

Eight

DAISY LAY IN BED, fuming at the curious activity taking place on the floor below without her. Despite what her parents said, she was no longer a child. She would be eighteen in six months and done with school. It would take more than some silly séance to give her nightmares. Not that it mattered. Her parents had made up their minds, and it was pointless to argue.

She glanced toward the window. Outside, the snow was falling thick and fast. A low moon hung in the sky, casting an oblong patch of pale light onto the floor. The house was silent and still. The younger children had gone to their beds with an equal amount of protestation but were now deep in the land of nod, no doubt.

Daisy wished she were so lucky. It was hard being Thomas Finch's daughter. She didn't know exactly what he did at work, but she suspected it was not a normal government job. He never spoke of what went on at his job, or why he sometimes spent days, and even weeks, away from home. Sometimes, when he returned, there was a haunted look behind his eyes. Sometimes, Daisy wondered if boarding school was merely a way to get her out of the house and away from whatever clandestine work her father was engaged in. Her mother didn't appear to know much more about that work than she did, although Daisy sometimes suspected her mother knew more than she was letting on.

And now this humiliation.

Being treated like a ten-year-old and sent to bed.

It was almost as if her father was unaware of Daisy's budding maturity and still viewed her as the prepubescent girl that played with dolls and spent her evenings reading fairytales about knights in shining armor and sleeping princesses. Her mother was no better, at least when her father was around. She deferred to him in almost all aspects of Daisy's upbringing, which drove the teenager wild with frustration. If her own mother didn't understand her, what hope was there?

Daisy shifted in bed and turned away from the window, fluffing the pillows up. She hunkered down under the covers, shivering against the cold winter air that permeated the room even though a dying fire burned in the small fireplace on the opposite wall.

She closed her eyes and tried to sleep, but the Sandman was elusive. Frustrated, Daisy shifted again and lay there staring at the ceiling.

Then she heard it.

A creak in the darkness.

Daisy held her breath and listened. Her heart pounded in her chest, sounding much too loud.

When the creak came again, she could take no more and sat up, holding the covers to her chest.

First, Daisy saw nothing amiss. The fire was slowly dying in the hearth. The snow was still falling outside the window. Her travel bag sat on a wingback chair in the corner of the room, nothing more than a vague outline in the darkness.

Then her eyes snapped toward the bedroom door.

Where it had been closed before, it now stood a few inches open.

Daisy's heart skipped a beat even as she tried to reason away the strange occurrence.

The house was old and drafty. Perhaps the door had blown open, or maybe it didn't catch properly when she went to bed and had merely swung back on its hinges.

But there had been no breeze in the hallway, and Daisy was sure she heard the latch click when she closed the door. Then another thought occurred to Daisy. Maybe it was her parents checking on her to make sure she had actually gone to bed.

"Hello," she called out in a soft voice. "Is anybody there?"

She received no answer.

Daisy waited a moment, her eyes still on the door. If it wasn't her parents who opened it, then who?

"Stop scaring yourself, Daisy," she said aloud, chastising herself for the wild thoughts that ran through her mind. "The door doesn't latch properly, that's all."

But even as she spoke the words, Daisy didn't believe them, because she had tugged on the handle after closing the door to make sure it was latched before she undressed for bed.

So maybe it had been her parents after all, and they had simply neglected to close it properly when they went back downstairs.

Daisy decided this was the most obvious explanation and slipped back down in bed. She closed her eyes again, focusing her thoughts on the upcoming festivities. She loved the Christmas season more than any because it was so full of happiness and joy. It was one of the few times of the year that her father shucked the weight of the world and relaxed.

A footstep broke the silence, then another. They were faint, but unmistakable.

Daisy's eyes snapped open.

She sat up in time to see the door swing wider on protesting hinges. The corridor beyond was dark and gloomy.

"Hello?" Daisy called again. The hairs on the back of her neck prickled.

For a second, all was silent, then the footsteps resumed, light and fast, sounding like... the footfalls of a child.

All at once, Daisy realized how foolish she had been. It wasn't her parents checking on her, or one of the ghosts Lady Elizabeth had spoken of at dinner. It was that boy, Eric. Or maybe his sister.

Daisy swung her legs off the bed and slipped out from under the covers. She grabbed a robe and pulled it around her nightgown to keep out the chill. She rushed to the open door and stepped out into the hallway beyond, just in time to see a flash of movement disappear around the corner toward the stairs—A young boy clad in a white nightshirt that billowed out behind him.

"Stop. Come back," she said in a half whisper, taking off after the fleeting and mysterious figure.

But when she got to the top of the stairs, there was no sign of the boy she had seen in the hallway. Daisy was alone.

Nine

DAISY STOOD at the top of the stairs and looked down at the floor below with a mixture of confusion and unease. She had seen the boy in the hallway as he turned the corner toward the stairs. How had he vanished so quickly and completely?

She lingered for a moment, confused, then turned to head back to her bedroom. Then, at the corner of her eye, she caught another flash of white.

There he was, in the grand entrance hall below, disappearing toward the back of the house. She started down the stairs, craning her neck over the rail but the briefly glimpsed figure was gone again, swallowed up in the darkness.

Daisy kept going, wishing she had brought the nightlight that sat next to her bed. It would have only taken a second to light the candle. But she hadn't and had no intention of going back for it now.

She reached the bottom of the stairs.

To her right was the library. The doors were closed but she could hear a faint voice that carried a thick accent from behind them. This must be Madame Serafina, the spirit medium Lady

Elizabeth had brought in for the séance. She had assumed that she was following the young boy, Eric, sneaking down to listen at the door. But instead of going to the library, the figure had gone the other way and vanished toward the back of the house. She could think of no reason for him to go there. The dining room was to her left. The drawing room was behind the library to her right. Both of them were empty. She didn't know what lay beyond that, but the kitchen must be close by, and maybe even a scullery. None of this should be of interest to a ten-year-old boy.

Daisy hesitated a moment, unsure what to do. The last thing she wanted was to be discovered roaming the house, but her curiosity was piqued. Just exactly what was the young boy up to, and where had he gone? Making up her mind, she turned left and skirted the staircase. There were two doors beyond the dining room on her right. When she peeked into the first she found a kitchen, just as expected. The second door was indeed a scullery, with an area for washing dishes and doing the laundry. A mangle, used to wring water from wet garments, stood in the corner. It looked to Daisy like some kind of medieval torture device.

At the back of the house, she found a semicircular conservatory with glass windows running all the way around. It overlooked the rear gardens, which were now blanketed in a heavy layer of snow. Wherever the boy had gone, he was not here.

Daisy left the conservatory behind and completed her circuit of the back of the house, arriving at what could only be Lord Percy's study, complete with an enormous oak desk upon which sat stacks of papers and several leather-bound volumes. The boy was not here either.

Next to the study was the drawing room.

Maybe the boy had snuck downstairs to open a present.

But this room was empty, too. The fire had burned down in the grate to nothing but glowing embers. The tree stood in the corner with all the gifts undisturbed beneath.

Puzzled, Daisy returned to the front of the house. The boy was nowhere to be found. Had he run in a circle and gone back upstairs even as she was searching below? That was the only thing that made sense, unless... she was following a ghost. Daisy dismissed this idea almost as soon as it occurred to her. There were no such things as ghosts. It was Eric playing pranks, nothing more. By now he would be diving back under the covers in his room and pretending to be asleep lest anyone check on him.

Daisy went back to the stairs, intending to return to her room, but then she turned and looked at the closed library doors. Her father had said she could not attend the séance, but she could still listen from outside in the entrance hall and no one would be any the wiser.

With a lump in her throat, Daisy crept back across the entrance hall toward the library. She pressed her ear to the door and listened.

Ten

WHEN THE CANDLES BLEW OUT, Eden gave a shrill scream. Breaking Decker's grip, her hand flew to her mouth. Across the table, Florence looked equally startled. Her gaze flitted between Madame Serafina and the floating candelabra, which was now nothing more than a vague silhouette in the darkness.

"Well, this just got interesting," Finch muttered under his breath.

Another voice floated out of the darkness. It was Madame Serafina. She spoke in a strangely lyrical tone, almost sing-song in its nature. "The spirits are close at hand."

Eden squealed.

Her husband, sitting on the other side of her, made an irritated sound. "Do try to control yourself, my dear."

"Silence," snapped Madame Serafina in a most un-trancelike way. A moment passed, then she continued in a voice more suitable to her theatrics. "Is there a spirit among us who wishes to communicate?"

A short, sharp knock answered the medium's question.

"Then speak, oh spirit, I implore you."

Almost immediately, an answer came from the other side of the room. The voice was low and guttural, with no trace of an accent. It almost sounded like a man, but not quite. "I am here to converse with Edward."

There was a sharp intake of breath from across the table.

"Edward, that sounds like your father," whispered Florence in a trembling voice.

"It sounds like nothing of the sort," Lark responded. "Who is this, and what do you want?"

"You don't recognize me, boy?"

"It is your father," Florence said. "Maybe he wants to apologize for treating you so badly while he was alive."

"Or maybe it's a bunch of balderdash. I don't believe in ghosts, and I certainly don't think my father would take the trouble to return from the spirit world just to say he was sorry for making my childhood a living hell."

"That's exactly why I came back, son." The voice had shifted. It sounded like it was coming from the other side of the room now, behind Lark. "I never meant all those things I said, and I'm sorry from the bottom of my heart. Can you ever forgive me so that I can pass over in peace?"

"If you're my father, what was my childhood nickname?"

"Son, I don't have time for such trivialities. I can only break the veil for a short time. I grow weak even as we talk."

"Edward, just forgive him," Florence implored. "He's your father."

"If that will make the man go away, then fine. I forgive him."

The voice was growing faint now. "Thank you, son. Always remember that I love you."

"That's definitely not my father," Edward said with a snort. "The man never said he loved me the whole time he was alive, so I can't imagine he'd bother now that he's dead."

The medium made a small moaning sound. Her head jerked up and her eyes snapped open. "He is gone back whence he came."

"Good riddance," muttered Edward.

Madame Serafina ignored the comment. Her head dropped once more, and her eyes fluttered closed. She swayed back and forth in her chair before becoming still again. "Another spirit wishes to step forward."

"This should be good," Edward whispered.

Florence nudged him. "Do be quiet and let someone else have a turn."

"Eden, my little girl. Look at you, all grown up," said a female voice from somewhere in the darkness to Decker's right. It sounded old and full of phlegm. "It is I."

Eden squealed with delight. "Grandmother. I never thought I'd hear from you again."

Decker resisted the urge to stand and explore the darkness because he knew what he would find. There would be nobody there, let alone a spirit. These voices were coming from the medium, Madame Serafina, he was sure. She was altering her voice and throwing it to make it sound like someone in another part of the room was speaking. If nothing else, she was a fantastic actress.

The conversation between Eden and her probably fake grandmother was still continuing. When it was over, Eden let out another squeal and proclaimed that she had never been so amazed in her entire life.

Decker wondered how many other disembodied relatives of those present would make themselves known, but apparently, Madame Serafina was now moving on to a more elaborate trickery.

The candelabra, which had floated effortlessly for the last

fifteen minutes, performed a slow pirouette, then dropped back to the table with a loud thud.

Everyone in the room jumped, and a couple of people let out startled exclamations. One of the unlit candles, shaken loose by the impact, fell onto the table.

A knock came from somewhere near Madame Serafina, drawing everyone's attention.

Eden gasped.

Florence tittered nervously.

Lily, sitting next to Finch, drew in a sharp breath.

The medium sat stiff and upright in her chair. Her eyes had taken on the appearance of saucers. Her hands were out of sight under the table. But it was the white billowing substance flowing from her mouth that had elicited so much surprise from the assembled guests.

"Give me a break," Finch muttered, leaning close to Decker. "There's no such thing as ectoplasm. This woman is going too far."

Decker said nothing. He was fascinated by this turn of events and was actually starting to have fun. It made a change from chasing real-life monsters and ghouls. The ectoplasm, he surmised, was probably nothing more than cotton or some other suitable material cleverly concealed somewhere about the medium's body and retrieved while the falling candelabra distracted those at the table. It was classic misdirection. The same technique magicians had been using for centuries.

"This is incredible," said Archibald Stour, apparently won over by this latest act of deception.

The ectoplasm finished oozing and disappeared under the table, where Madame Serafina's hands rested, conveniently placed to conceal it once more. Before anyone could question where the mysterious substance had gone, her eyes fluttered again and closed. She raised her arms into the air, black-gloved hands almost invisible in the darkness, and tilted her head back. "If there are any further spirits who wish to communicate. I order you to come forth at this time."

Everyone held their breath, waiting for what would occur next.

Ten seconds passed, then fifteen.

Madame Serafina nodded as if she was listening to some voice only she could hear. Then she drew a deep breath and opened her mouth to speak again.

But before she could utter a word, the doorbell clanged three times from the entrance hall beyond the library.

Eleven

DAISY WAS STILL STANDING at the door, listening to the events on the other side, when the doorbell rang. It was so unexpected that she almost jumped out of her skin.

She froze, caught in a moment of indecision.

It was past midnight, much too late for a visitor to be calling upon the household. Not only that, but the snowstorm had grown worse. She had seen the blizzard churning outside the window when she poked her head into the drawing room. How could anyone even have made it up the long driveway to the manor house, let alone be standing on the front stoop ringing the doorbell?

Then her instincts took over. Any moment now, the library doors would open, and everyone would spill out, including her parents, to see who was calling at such an inappropriate time. The Butler, Davies, might have heard the bell as well, although he was probably tucked up in bed on the third floor under the sloping roof where the staff quarters were located. Not that it mattered. Someone would answer, and then she would be caught.

Daisy looked around, frantic for somewhere to hide, but the grand entrance hall was a vast open expanse with only a few pieces of furniture and nothing large enough to conceal her. There was only one thing for it. She turned and sprinted toward the stairs just as the library doors opened. There was no time to reach the second floor and her bedroom. She veered to the right, skirting the stairs, and ran toward the back of the house instead, then ducked into the open space underneath the stairs and stopped, breathless, in the nick of time. Another few seconds and someone would have spotted her, for sure.

She crossed under the stairs to the other side, where she could see the library and pushed herself back into the darkness, hoping no one would notice her.

The library doors opened, and Lady Elizabeth appeared with her husband. The guests filed out behind. Daisy saw her parents and their friend, John Decker. No one looked her way, for which she was grateful. The last person to leave the library was Madame Serafina, her black dress trailing the floor. She still wore the scarf around her head but had added black gloves that covered her arms to the sleeves of her dress.

She looks like the angel of death, Daisy thought, hovering to snatch an unwary soul.

An involuntary shudder ran through her.

Everyone was moving toward the front door. Hushed conversations passed between the group—speculation regarding who might call so late. They moved across the grand entrance hall and out of Daisy's field of view. She edged forward, slipping noiselessly from her hiding place to gain a better angle. Hunkering low, she moved along the side of the staircase and stopped, peering through the balusters, ready to drop back out of sight should anyone glance her way.

Lady Elizabeth was at the front door.

Her husband, Lord Percy, stood at her right shoulder. "Well?

Go on then, open it and let's see who the devil is out on such a horrible night," he said.

"Maybe it's some poor traveler who got lost in the storm," Eden said, craning her neck to see past her host.

"Or maybe some crazy person escaped from the lunatic asylum," said the banker, Fitzmorris.

"Don't say that." Eden's voice trembled. "You're scaring me."

"I think we're safe enough. There are no lunatic asylums within walking distance of here," Percy said. "Especially not in weather such as this."

"Open the door and let's find out," Lark said. "The suspense is unbearable."

Lady Elizabeth reached out and gripped the door handle.

Daisy held her breath. What if it was an escaped lunatic? Would that madman lunge forward with a hideous shriek the moment lady Elizabeth opened the door, clawing and swiping at whoever was close enough to endure their wrath? She knew it was implausible but was unable to contain a frisson of unease. After all, were not such random events the staple of Christmas ghost stories that had become so popular? She would soon find out.

Lady Elizabeth hesitated a moment, then pulled the door open before taking a quick step backward in anticipation of who or what might wait on the other side.

Snow swirled through the open doorway, driven by a howling wind that whipped through the porte-cochère. But of the visitor who came to Blackthorn Manor and rang the bell on such an inhospitable evening, lunatic or otherwise, Daisy saw no sign.

Twelve

PERCY STEPPED around his wife and peered out into the snow-laden night. "Well, I'll be darned. No one is there."

"Someone must have been there," Lady Elizabeth commented. "We all heard the bell ring."

"Maybe they left before we had a chance to answer," said the businessman, Archibald Stour. He rubbed his hands and blew on them. "Rather inconsiderate, if you ask me. It's letting all the heat out of the house."

"I agree, old chap. The least you could do is hang around once you've rung someone's bell." Fitzmorris tapped the businessman on the back. "To not do so is beyond rude."

"Especially at such a time of night," Stour replied.

"They didn't leave again." Percy stepped past his wife and looked down at the snow-covered ground with a puzzled expression.

There, clearly visible in the fallen snow, was a set of footprints leading from the driveway, up the steps, to the front door. Footsteps that began only fifteen feet from the house. Beyond that was nothing but a blanket of uninterrupted, pristine whiteness. No footsteps. No carriage tracks. Nothing. It was as if their visitor had dropped from the sky along with the still-falling snowflakes. But as if that were not enough, the lack of footprints leading away from the door again was just as baffling. Whoever had rung the bell should still be there.

"Well, that's ruddy unusual." Stour pushed his way forward, stared at the vanishing footprints, then turned to Lady Elizabeth. "My compliments to you on your cleverness. To conclude the séance with this ghostly finale... Brilliant."

"I assure you, Archie, this puzzling turn of events has nothing to do with either myself or my husband."

"Come now, Lizzie, don't be so bashful." Stour grinned. "How did you do it?"

"I bet they had a maid sneak around to the front of the house and ring the doorbell," said Lark. "Or maybe that butler of theirs, Davies."

"The staff have all retired for the night," Lady Elizabeth said. "Whoever approached our door did not originate from within this house. I promise you that. The doorbell surprised me as much as it did the rest of you."

"But it must have been the staff. Nothing else makes sense."

"Then how did they avoid leaving footprints until they were right in front of the door?" Eden asked, looking more terrified than amused.

"A good question," said her husband.

"All the best magic tricks are hard to explain. Just look at the floating candelabra." Lark glanced back toward the library. "Baffling."

Decker thought he knew how the candelabra had lifted from the table. It was a simple matter of rigging invisible wires, which, no doubt, the butler had done while preparing the room for Madame Serafina's séance. The other supernatural events that occurred in the library would have been similarly staged, such as the sudden breeze and the spectral voices that appeared to come from other areas of the room. He suspected Davies had not, in fact, retired for the night but was complicit in the charade. Even now, with the guests suitably distracted, he might be removing the evidence of trickery back in the library. The doorbell and footsteps in the snow might just be part of the evening's entertainment. But something nagged at him. Lady Elizabeth appeared genuinely surprised by this turn of events, as did her husband. "What do you think?" He asked, leaning close to Finch and whispering.

"I'm as clueless as you, I'm afraid." Finch stood with his arms folded, his gaze resting on the doorway. "Try as I might, I cannot think of any way to reach the point at which the footprints begin without leaving some evidence in the snow prior to that."

"I agree." It did, at first, seem impossible, even to Decker. But wasn't that the point of such trickery? Or maybe Blackthorn Manor really was haunted, and they had just been visited by one of its spectral denizens.

"This is getting us nowhere, and it's freezing outside," Percy grumbled. "Lizzie, close the door."

"But Percy, someone must have rung the doorbell. Maybe they need help."

"Goodness, woman. You can see there's no one anywhere in sight." Percy frowned and stepped out into the snow. "But if it makes you happy, I'll look around."

"I'll help," Lark said, joining him.

"Me too. This is all frightfully entertaining," Fitzmorris said with a chuckle.

They ventured out under the porte-cochère, their footsteps crunching on the windblown snow as they descended the steps to the driveway, careful to avoid the strange footprints that had appeared out of nowhere. They trudged around for a couple of minutes, walking back and forth in front of the house before regrouping.

Percy turned back to his wife. "See. There's no one here. We are well and truly alone."

"Let's go back inside." Lark rubbed his hands together. "I vote we retire to the drawing room and have ourselves a brandy to warm our bones before we turn in for the night."

"An excellent idea." Fitzmorris started back toward the house.

"William, it's one o'clock in the morning," said Eden as her husband stepped back inside.

"Just a snifter," he replied.

"What about the séance?" Elizabeth asked, looking disappointed. "We haven't finished yet."

"I think we've had quite enough of that." Percy closed the front door, brushed snowflakes from his shoulders, and then turned to his wife. "You should rouse a maid to attend Madame Serafina. She won't be able to head back to the city tonight in such foul weather. I doubt her carriage will even make it down the driveway."

"Very well." Elizabeth sighed. She turned to the medium. "Will that be agreeable with you, Madame Serafina?"

"I have no desire to venture out into the storm tonight," Serafina replied, her accent sounding less pronounced now. "To tell the truth, I have become rather lightheaded in the last few minutes and would welcome the opportunity to lie down."

"Oh, dear. I hope it's nothing serious," lady Elizabeth said, looking concerned.

"I'm sure it is nothing. Just a gentle chill." Madame Serafina patted her brow with a handkerchief pulled from her pocket.

"Maybe the ghost rang the doorbell, letting you know it's still around." Fitzmorris laughed nervously.

"Stop. You give me the chills," his wife said with a shudder.

"I'm sure it's no ghost. I shall call for a maid immediately, and we'll have you settled in no time." Elizabeth turned away from the front door, then stopped, letting out a small murmur of surprise.

Eric and Celia, the two children, were standing on the stairs watching the proceedings.

"What are you doing out of bed?" asked Florence, tutting.

"We heard a noise," Eric replied. "It woke us up."

"Someone was in our room." Celia glanced nervously back toward the top of the stairs. "I heard them open the door and walk in. I think it was the little boy Lady Elizabeth told us about at dinner."

"It was nothing of the sort," said Lark. "You had nightmares just like I thought you would. Now, go back to bed."

"He was there," Eric protested. "I know it was him."

"Nonsense."

"But—"

"Enough of this foolishness." Florence pointed toward the top of the stairs. "Do as your father told you."

At first, the children didn't move, but then they turned and made their way back upstairs.

Lark watched them go; then he clapped his hands together. "All right, then. How about that nightcap?"

Thirteen

DAISY WAITED until the children had retreated to their bedrooms, the adults to the drawing room, and Madame Serafina had followed a maid upstairs, before she crept out from the dark space under the stairs where she had sequestered herself upon fear of discovery.

Curious, she padded to the front door, glanced over her shoulder to ensure she was not being observed, and opened it silently. The footsteps were still there, although partially obliterated near the door by Percy and his friends when they had stepped outside to render potential aid to the phantom visitor. But they were quickly losing their definition as fresh snow fell on top of them. In a couple of hours, there would be nothing left of the footprints but slight depressions, if anything at all.

Still, she could see where the footprints began, and it was curious. It appeared as if the person who made them had materialized in the middle of the driveway and then walked toward the house before ringing the doorbell and vanishing. Regardless of the consensus among the dinner guests that it was a cleverly contrived end to the séance perpetrated by Lady Elizabeth, Daisy could see no means by which such a feat could be accomplished. It was, she thought, simply impossible and certainly beyond the talents of the butler, Davies, and the rest of the household stuff.

From across the grand entrance hall, in the direction of the drawing room, came muffled voices and an occasional peel of laughter. Deep in the house, a clock struck one, the single chime sounding forlorn as it echoed through the old house.

Daisy shuddered and pushed the door closed, careful not to let it slam. She turned toward the grand staircase and stood there, thinking about the wraithlike figure she had chased from her bedroom. She had assumed it to be the boy, Eric, up to no good. Now she was not so sure. How could he possibly have made it back upstairs without her noticing, only to reappear later with his sister when the doorbell rang? But if it was not Eric that had roused her from the bedchamber, then who?

An unsettling thought rattled through her mind.

Perhaps it was the ghost of that boy that vanished a hundred years ago and was never found. A boy probably about the same age as Eric, who perhaps snuck down in a similar fashion, aggrieved at being sent to bed before he was ready. She shook the creepy sentiment off. The ghost stories were nothing more than that. Stories. Lady Elizabeth was renowned for her hijinks at Christmas. Her parties were known throughout the Home Counties and beyond. She had probably made up the ghost stories in preparation for the séance she knew would follow at midnight. After all, who would purchase and restore a haunted house of their own free will when they were aware of the restless spirits that roamed within? Nobody would, thought Daisy, as she made her way back across the hall to the foot of the stairs.

Another burst of raucous laughter erupted from the drawing room. The adults were showing no sign of retreating to bed anytime soon. Daisy glanced toward the library where the séance had occurred. She considered sneaking inside to see what all the fuss was about but then thought better of it. What would there be to see, anyway? The séance was over, and Madame Serafina had gone to bed. Any events of interest had already occurred, and she knew what a stuffy old library looked like. They had a library at her boarding school, and this one would probably not be any different except smaller.

Daisy started back up the stairs, walking as close to the balustrade as possible to avoid any creaky treads. She reached the top and turned around, giving the grand entrance hall below a last lingering glance before heading back to her room. Her thoughts turned again to the strange figure who had pushed her door open and fled, leading her downstairs and through the house, only to vanish as if it had never been there... Just like whoever rang the doorbell.

A shudder wormed its way up Daisy's spine. She wished she were back home in London, safely tucked up in her own warm and comfortable bedroom, rather than this creepy old mansion in the middle of the countryside.

The room was dark when she stepped inside. The fire had burned itself to nothing but angry red embers, and the temperature had dropped enough that she could see her breath in the air when she exhaled. She went to the fireplace, put more kindling in the grate, and took a log from the small rack nearby. Picking up the poker, she sifted the red-hot embers until the kindling caught alight, then fanned the flames until they licked around the log. She stood warming herself for a few minutes, aware that the small hearth would do little but take the edge off the chill once she stepped away from its vicinity.

But she could not stand in front of the fire all night. Reluctantly, Daisy returned to the bed, took off her robe, and climbed under the covers, pulling them up to her chin.

She lay there, listening to the crackle of the fire and hoping she would not hear the strange footsteps again in the hallway or see her door swing slowly open on squeaky hinges.

A tiny whimper escaped her throat.

She slid down under the covers, dragging the pillow with her, and pulled them up over her head, then closed her eyes and tried to sleep, hoping the ghosts of Blackthorn Manor would be swept away come daylight.

Fourteen

IN THE DRAWING ROOM, Lord Percy handed out snifters to the men and Sherry glasses to the women. He went around the room, filling them with great delight from a pair of bottles clutched in his hands. He returned the liquor to a globe-shaped cabinet sitting in the corner of the room and raised his glass with a glint in his eye. "To a most enthralling and entertaining evening," he said, toasting the room.

"Hear, hear," said Stour, raising his own glass. "I don't think I've had so much fun since your New Year's Eve party in London two years ago. The ghostly theme of the night was absolutely perfect, and the séance a more than fitting end to the evening, even if you won't take credit for that darned clever distraction with the doorbell."

"Those footsteps, and our vanishing visitor, were nothing to do with either myself or Percy," Lady Elizabeth said with slight irritation. "I don't know how many more times I have to protest my innocence."

"Regardless, it was a mighty fine jape."

"I think it was rather horrid," said Eden. "I practically swooned with fear. What if someone really needed our help and they are out there even now in that blizzard, all alone and freezing to death?"

"Now, Eden, there is nobody lost outside in the storm," Fitzmorris said, putting an arm around his wife to reassure her. "If there was, we would have seen them. I'm with Archie. It was all a wonderful prank played on us by our hosts, who are even now trying to convince us that they are innocent on all counts."

"It seems that I shall never convince any of you that those footprints in the snow were genuine, so instead, I'm giving in. You may believe whatever you want." Lady Elizabeth shook her head in frustration and finished her sherry. She turned and approached the liquor cabinet and poured herself another drink. "I'm just sorry that the séance was interrupted and brought to an early conclusion."

Decker glanced at Finch, who was standing next to Lily, observing the conversation with wordless interest. He drew him to one side and leaned close. "What do you make of it all?"

"I think lady Elizabeth has outdone herself, as usual," Finch said. "The séance was rigged, naturally, but that did not detract from the overall fun."

"And the footsteps in the snow?" Decker asked. "What do you make of those?"

"My dear boy, stop looking for supernatural occurrences around every corner." Finch sipped his drink. "Lady Elizabeth is notoriously cagey about her trickery, which is what makes her parties so special. This wouldn't be the first time she's refused to own up to a prank. If she did, it would spoil the mystery, don't you think?"

"I can see no earthly way she could have pulled off such a feat."

"Which is what makes it so jolly." Finch sighed. "I know what we do for work, but for one night of the year, relax and enjoy yourself."

"And if our disappearing guest does turn out to be supernatural in nature?"

"Then it's a harmless manifestation and I see no need to get involved." Finch smiled thinly. "Maybe Lizzie is right, and this house is haunted. It wouldn't be the first time we have run across such a thing. In this case, though, I see no danger to anyone, and the fact remains that Lizzie is most likely behind everything."

Decker lapsed into silence. He was well aware that ghosts were real. He had come up against not just ghosts, but a particularly nasty entity of nonhuman origin only a month before in the small country village of Mavendale. Of course, that particular assignment had resulted in the disappearance of a young woman he considered almost like a daughter. Despite a frantic search in the weeks since then, they had still not located Mina. He took a swig of his drink and forced the thoughts from his mind. It would do no good to dwell on the situation and he had promised himself on the ride here that he would not become morose regarding his current circumstances. Finch wanted to distract him, and Decker was grateful for that distraction.

The party was winding down now.

The drinks were running low, and the conversation was waning. Everyone was tired.

Eden yawned and nudged her husband. "I think it's time we went to bed, darling."

"Yes, of course." Fitzmorris bade everyone a good night and withdrew with his wife at his side.

The businessman, Archibald Stour, was next. He gulped the last of his drink and placed the glass on the low table between the couches before heading toward the stairs.

Decker could see no point in lingering any longer. He put his own half-finished drink down and said good night to Thomas Finch and Lily, then followed Stour and climbed up to the second floor.

The hallway leading to his bedroom was dimly lit by a pair of glowing wall sconces. Back in London, the grandest homes were already being electrified, but here in the country, most dwellings still relied upon candles and oil lamps. Blackthorn Manor was one of the few places hereabouts to have gas lamps thanks to Lord Percy's recent renovation and what Decker surmised was a very expensive gas line running from the town of Chelmsford several miles away.

Edward Lark and his wife Florence were coming up the stairs behind him. Decker could hear them talking in soft tones. Upon reaching the landing, they turned the other way toward the east wing of the house and soon their voices faded away.

Decker arrived at his bedroom door and turned the knob. He expected it would open easily, but it didn't. The same thing happened when he tried a second time. He rattled the handle, wondering if the latch was jammed, but still the door did not open. Stepping back, Decker observed the door, confused. He hadn't locked it when he left to go downstairs earlier. In fact, he didn't even have a key. The only explanation was that the rapidly falling temperature outside had caused the door to swell and jam. He tried one last time, putting his shoulder against the door to force it open, but it stubbornly refused to budge.

Cursing under his breath, Decker turned back toward the stairs, hoping that Lord Percy was still in the drawing room.

He had only gone a few steps when a low creak drew his attention.

Decker turned back to the door and was surprised to find it now standing ajar. Perplexed, but grateful, he returned to the bedroom and stepped inside. Perhaps his attempts to open it had loosened the door, or maybe he was just over-tired. Either way, it didn't matter. Tomorrow, he would let Percy know about the sticking door, but right now, all he wanted was his bed.

Fifteen

DECKER AWOKE IN THE DARKNESS, his eyes snapping open.

The figure stood at the end of the bed, nothing but a small, vague outline against the gloom.

Decker's breath caught in his throat. He lay unmoving, his gaze fixed on the strange, childlike apparition. Even though he could see no eyes, or any facial features, Decker sensed the figure staring back at him, too. Then it raised an arm, extending a crooked finger toward the bedroom door.

Outside, somewhere in the snowy night, the faint hoot of an owl broke the silence, its call loaded with melancholy.

Decker's gaze flicked to the window, drawn by the sorrowful cry. When he looked back, the figure was gone.

He sat up, startled, reaching for the bedside lamp before he realized that there wasn't one. In fact, there were no light fixtures in the bedroom at all. Just a handheld nightlight with a single candle sitting next to the bed. There was a box of matches there, too. He picked them up and drew one out, fumbling to light it, then touched the flame to the candle's wick. A soft yellow glow pushed at the darkness, struggling to vanquish the night.

Decker glanced sideways toward the fireplace, where red glowing embers simmered. The room felt cold. Freezing. Outside, snow was still coming down. A thin sheen of ice clung to the windowpanes.

Decker stared at the spot where the apparition had appeared. Had he really seen the somber figure, or was it merely the remnant of an uneasy dream that lingered into wakefulness? He decided it must have merely been his own overactive imagination conjuring up phantoms where none existed.

The house was silent. His wristwatch, on the stand next to the burning nightlight, read three a.m.

Decker snuffed out the candle and slid back down under the covers, pulling them up against the chill air.

He closed his eyes.

The owl hooted a second time, further away now.

Sleep pushed at the edges of Decker's mind. He drifted off, warm in the bed, until...

The sound of footsteps reached his ears, light and furtive. They came from the hallway outside his door. Decker opened his eyes again and sat back up. He strained to listen, and at first heard nothing, but then came another shuffle of feet as if someone were creeping around in the night.

Decker jumped up and snatched his robe from the end of the bed, pulling it around him and cinching the belt. He picked up the nightlight, lit it, and went to the door, easing it open and peering into the darkness beyond.

The hallway was empty.

Decker opened the door further and stepped out. The wall sconces that lit the passageway were off now. Inky blackness swirled around, doing its best to defeat the glow from his candle.

He glanced over his shoulder toward the other bedrooms,

but the doors were closed. As far as he could tell, the house was asleep.

More footsteps. Faint but recognizable. They came from the other direction, near the stairs. Decker held his breath and strained to listen, wondering if one of the children had slipped from their room to go exploring.

The creak of a stair tread.

Decker took off down the corridor. He reached the top of the stairs and peered down, but saw no one. The grand entrance hall was empty. Yet the feeling persisted that he was not alone.

"Is anyone there?" he called in a low voice.

A few seconds passed in silence. Then, out of the darkness, a barely audible giggle.

A shudder ran through Decker. He started down the stairs, determined to find the origin of the unsettling laugh. At the bottom, he stopped again and held the nightlight high, looking around, but saw no one.

To his right, the library doors stood open. Decker stepped inside. The table upon which Madame Serafina had conducted her séance was gone. So was the candelabra. Decker glanced toward the ceiling, wondering if he would see any remnants of the wires that must have been used to levitate it, but he saw no sign. Someone, probably the butler, Davies, had done a good job of cleaning up. Bookcases heavy with somber volumes clad the walls from floor to ceiling. Many of the books looked old. Decker wondered if they had come along with the house or if Lord Percy brought them with him.

Decker stepped out of the library and went to the next door. The drawing room was similarly empty and dark.

He retreated to the grand entrance hall, intending to cross over to the dining room, and searched there. But he didn't get a chance.

More footsteps. Like socks on the wood floor.

They came from somewhere behind the sweeping staircase. He set off again, making his way to the back of the house. The conservatory doors stood open. He stepped inside and came to a stop, the tenebrous space falling away all around him. The room's walls comprised large windows that curved around on a metal skeleton. The glass ceiling above him was heavy with snow. Outside, the landscape was sheathed in white. More snow was still falling, but not as hard now. Decker half expected to see more footsteps cutting through the flat expanse, mysteriously picking up then ending of their own volition, with no clue to their maker. But there were none. The wintry scene beyond the windows was undisturbed and pristine.

He looked around the conservatory. A grand piano occupied one side of the space. A sofa and two chairs stood nearby. Tall plants in pots stood at intervals. Decker gave the room one more glance, then returned to the main house.

He was about to set off back toward the grand entrance hall when the patter of footsteps once again reached his ears.

They were closer now. Right behind him.

Decker swiveled. The candle flickered in its holder and almost blew out. A figure wrapped in pale fabric loomed out of the darkness. Decker took a quick step back, alarmed.

Then the figure spoke.

Sixteen

"MR. DECKER, what are you doing down here?"

"I could ask you the same question," Decker said, looking at Daisy, who was standing before him dressed in a flowing nightgown and white robe. "Why are you creeping around in the middle of the night?"

"Probably for the same reason you are," Daisy replied. "Something woke me up. Footsteps in the hallway. It's not the first time, either. I heard them earlier and came down to investigate while you were all in the séance. I saw someone, too. It looked like a small boy. I thought it was Eric, so I followed him, but when I got down here, the boy had vanished."

An image of the figure standing at the end of his bed flashed through Decker's mind. Now that he thought about it, the figure had a certain boy-like quality. He thought it was merely the lingering residue of a forgotten dream dragged into the real world. Now he was not so sure. "What did the boy look like?"

Daisy shrugged. "I don't know. Didn't get a good look at him. All I saw was a fleeting glimpse."

"And he led you down here?"

"Yes. I was about to go back upstairs when the doorbell rang. Almost bowled me over with fright."

"Did you see anyone in the entrance hall?" Decker asked. "Anyone who might have been responsible?"

"No. I was alone until the library doors opened and you all came out. Funny thing is, the boy I followed couldn't have been Eric, even though that's what I thought at the time. He came down after the doorbell rang and was wearing a completely different color nightshirt. Plus, I can't see how he could have crept back upstairs without me seeing."

"And then you heard footsteps again, just now. That's why you came back down?"

"Yes. I know everyone thinks that Lady Elizabeth's ghost stories at dinner are just that—stories—but I'm not so sure. Do you believe this house really is haunted, Mr. Decker? Are we chasing ghosts?"

"I don't know," Decker admitted. He hated to think that Thomas Finch had brought him to a house full of restless spirits, and on Christmas no less, but he was having a hard time believing that Lord Percy and Lady Elizabeth were behind such an elaborate ruse. They had rigged the séance, for sure. Decker didn't believe for one moment that Madame Serafina, with her levitating candelabras, faked voices, and phantom knockings, could really conjure the dead, but that didn't mean they weren't here.

"I don't like it down here," Daisy said with a grimace. "In fact, I don't like this house at all. It has a weird atmosphere."

"Come on," Decker said, nodding toward the stairs. "I don't think we're going to find anything else down here tonight. As you said, we're probably just chasing ghosts. Let's go back to bed and figure this out in the morning."

"Sounds good to me."

Together, they made their way back to the front of the house and up the grand staircase. They climbed in silence. At the top, Decker cast one more furtive glance over his shoulder toward the entrance hall below, but of the mysterious figure that had led them from their bedchambers, there was no sign.

He escorted Daisy back to her room.

She stepped inside and turned back to him before closing the door. "Please don't tell my parents about this," she begged. "I'm pretty sure my father wouldn't approve of me sneaking around in the dead of night."

"I'll let you in on a secret," Decker said with a smile. "He wouldn't approve of me doing it, either."

Daisy laughed at this. "Good night, Mr. Decker."

"Good night Daisy. And if you get the urge to do any more nocturnal exploring, come and find me first. I'm just two doors down on the left."

"I'll do that." Daisy closed the door, leaving Decker alone in the hallway.

He returned to his own room and set the nightlight down, removed his robe, then climbed into bed and blew out the candle.

After that, he lay there for the longest time, thinking about what had just occurred and wondering if their phantom visitor would make another appearance.

Seventeen

THE REST of the night passed without further incident. When Decker rose the next morning, he found the snow had stopped falling. The grounds outside his window looked like a scene from a Christmas card. He could see the private chapel off to his left. The stained-glass windows caught the sunlight and shined through, casting a kaleidoscope of color across the smooth white ground. A copse of evergreens further afield stood draped in a thick blanket of snow.

He dressed quickly and went downstairs. Everyone had gathered in the dining room, where breakfast was being served. When he entered, Daisy looked up at him, a subtle half smile playing on her lips, and motioned for him to take a chair to her right.

When he sat down, she turned to him with an impish look on her face. "I hope you slept well, Mr. Decker."

"About as well as could be expected," he replied, reaching toward the serving platters in the middle of the table and helping himself to eggs, bacon, bangers, and fried potato, which he piled onto his plate. "And you?"

"Like a baby." Daisy grinned.

Davies appeared and offered Decker a choice between tea and coffee. He chose coffee, waited for the butler to serve him, and then dug into his food.

As the meal drew to a close, the children, Eric and Celia, jumped up from the table.

"Can we go play?" Eric asked with an expected glance toward his mother.

"That's fine. But make sure you stay inside the house," said Florence. "And don't get into any mischief."

"We won't," Eric called over his shoulder, already dashing toward the grand entrance hall.

Celia followed him out, and they soon disappeared, footsteps echoing on the tile floor as they ran deeper into the house.

After breakfast, everyone returned to the conservatory, where they sat and conversed. Percy had recently purchased a phonograph which he brought out and played a variety of music.

Madame Serafina had not yet departed. Even though the snow had stopped falling, the driveway was still too treacherous for her carriage, and had reluctantly agreed to stay, even though she originally intended to be back in London before Christmas Day.

Decker had visited the library and found a book that he intended to read, but soon found Daisy hovering above him.

"There's a chessboard on the table over by the window. Do you play?" She asked expectantly.

"Not for many years," Decker admitted. His mother had taught him the game when he was a child, and he had continued playing after her untimely death. In college, he was a member of the chess club, and although he was a competent player, he never considered himself especially skilled. Now, after more than two decades, he wondered how worthy an opponent he would prove to be.

"I challenge you to a game," she said with a grin.

"Are you sure about that?" Decker said. "I'm bound to be rusty."

"I'll go easy on you." Daisy folded her arms. "Unless you're afraid of being beaten by a girl?"

"I'm afraid of no such thing." Decker smiled and laid his book down. He stood up. "Let's go."

Daisy led him to the chessboard, and they settled down on opposite sides. Because he controlled the white pieces, she let him make the first move—which she claimed gave him an advantage —bringing the king's pawn forward two spaces. Decker found himself checkmated fourteen moves later, much to Daisy's glee. A second game led to a similar outcome, by which time Decker suspected his chances of winning against her were practically none.

"Best out of five?" Daisy asked with a grin.

"That means I will have to beat you three times in a row." Decker shook his head. "I don't see that happening."

"I'll go easy on you." Daisy was already placing the pieces back on the board in their starting positions. "Since you have had little luck in the last two games, how about I start the next one?"

"Be my guest," Decker said. As he suspected, it didn't matter. Fifteen minutes later, he lost his third game. Forty minutes after that, he was down five to zero and unwilling to lose a sixth. Luckily, Davies appeared and announced that it was time for lunch, which would comprise finger foods and be served in the conservatory.

It was two o'clock in the afternoon.

Florence called for the children, who had been absent since

breakfast but received no answer. Irritated, she set off into the main house to search for them.

Finch approached Decker and looked down at the chessboard. "I see you got well and truly drubbed."

"He lost all five games," Daisy said gleefully. "I even gave him a couple of freebies and he still lost."

"I warned you I haven't played in a while." Decker stood and stepped away from the chessboard.

Finch chuckled. "Don't worry, old chap. She beats me every time we play, as well. She must get her talent for cunning from her mother."

"I'm just naturally gifted," Daisy said, then she made her way toward the platters of food Davies had placed on the grand piano's lid, and around which the other guests were already congregating.

Decker was about to follow when Florence reappeared with Celia at her side, but not her son. She looked worried.

"I can't find Eric, and he isn't answering when I call for him," she said.

"He probably just wandered off in a world of his own," Lark said, turning to his wife with a sandwich in his hand. "You know what he's like—always daydreaming."

"Edward, I'm serious. I've looked everywhere."

"Surely Celia knows where he is. After all, they were together." Lark approached his daughter. "Well?"

She shook her head. "We weren't together."

"What? Why the devil not?"

"We were playing hide and seek," Celia said in a small voice. She looked up at her father. "I wanted to hide first, but Eric said no. They were going to hide, and I should count to one hundred then come looking for them."

"They?" Lark asked, alarmed. He glanced around the room

to see if anyone else was missing. No one was. "Who was Eric with, Celia?"

A hush had fallen among the assembled guests. They edged forward to see what Celia would say next.

She looked up at her father as if the question was redundant. Then she answered, "Why, the other boy, of course!"

Eighteen

FOR A MOMENT, no one spoke, then lady Elizabeth shook her head. "There are no other children in the house."

"Yes, there are," Celia said. "We've been playing with him."

"You mean like an imaginary friend," Lark said, kneeling in front of his daughter. "Is that right?"

Celia hesitated, scrunching her face as if thinking, then shook her head slowly. "He's not imaginary. He's our friend."

"Celia, tell us the truth," Florence said, her voice cracking. "You won't be in trouble. Where is Eric?"

"I told you already, I don't know. We were playing hide and seek, and Eric went with the boy to hide first. I counted like they told me too, then went to look for them. I was searching for them so long I was getting bored. I was about to give up. Then I heard you calling for me."

"And before that?"

"We were in our bedroom upstairs playing Pirate and Traveler."

"It's a board game we brought with us to amuse the children," Florence said by way of explanation. "Eric loves it. He's into all things that have to do with pirates."

"I like it, too, but not as much," Celia said. "We had just finished one game and were going to start another when the boy came back. He asked us to play hide and seek instead."

"When you say the boy came back, what do you mean?" Florence asked. "Have you seen him before?"

Celia nodded. "He came into our room last night when we were sleeping and scared us. We told you, remember?"

Decker thought back to the night before when the doorbell had rung, and there was no one there. When they turned around, the children were standing at the bottom of the stairs. He had dismissed the claim of being visited by a ghostly child, but after his own experiences the previous night, he was beginning to wonder.

Florence, on the other hand, was far from convinced. "You had a bad dream, that's all."

"No. It wasn't a dream. After we went back to bed, the boy came into our room again. He asked if we wanted to be his friends. We were scared at first, but he didn't hurt us, so Eric said yes."

"This is ridiculous," Lark said, standing back up. "I'm wasting no more time on this foolishness. We need to find Eric."

"He's probably still hiding," Florence said. "You know what he gets like when he's playing."

"We'll search the house, then," Lady Elizabeth said. "I'm sure everyone will help."

"He can't have gone far," Percy said. "The house is big, but it's not that large."

Decker turned to Finch. "A word in private?"

Finch observed him for a moment, then nodded. He followed Decker to the other side of the room, near the chessboard. "What's on your mind?"

"The boy Celia claims has been visiting her and her brother. I'm not so sure they imagined him."

"Heavens. This is supposed to be a relaxing holiday weekend, not another day on the job. What makes you think this young boy is real?"

"Because I might have seen him myself last night." Decker explained his strange encounter in the bedroom—the pointing figure that had appeared at the end of his bed—and the footsteps that had drawn him from his room and led him downstairs. He did not, however, mention finding Daisy downstairs, having been disturbed by the same ghostly footfalls, because he didn't want to get her in trouble.

Finch listened with a blank expression on his face. When Decker finished talking, he rubbed his chin. "I don't know. What possible agenda could a ghostly boy have to lead Eric off in such a fashion?"

"We find that out, and we'll probably find Eric," Decker replied.

"You think this spirit is dangerous?"

"I don't have enough information to make a determination either way." Decker had sensed no malevolence during his encounter in the early hours of the morning, but that meant little. He wondered what Daisy's take on it was, given that she had also claimed to see the spirit.

"Ladies and gentlemen," Lord Percy said, holding up the brandy glass he had been drinking from and clinking the side of it with a fork to get everyone's attention and interrupting Decker's conversation with Finch. He waited for all eyes to turn his way before continuing. "It appears that young Eric has gone and gotten himself lost somewhere in the house. Let's give the place a thorough going over and find him, shall we? Then we can continue with our lunch. I'm sure it will not take long."

"Thank you," Florence said, looking relieved. She took her

daughter's hand. "You're going to stay right beside me while we find your brother."

"We should tell the staff, too," Lady Elizabeth said. "Maybe one of them saw Eric looking for a place to hide."

"A good idea." Percy motioned to Davies, who had taken up a position by the door with his hands behind his back after laying out the lunch.

"Very good, sir," the butler nodded and stepped from the room to inform the remaining household staff of the situation.

"We should check the grounds and chapel, too," said lady Elizabeth. "Maybe he went outside."

"Would anyone like to volunteer?" Percy asked, looking around the group.

When no one else responded, Decker raised his hand. "I'll check the grounds and search the chapel."

"I'll go with him," Daisy said, stepping forward.

"Absolutely not." Lily shot her daughter a concerned look. "It's freezing out there. You'll catch your death."

"Mother, I'm perfectly capable of going outside in the snow. Stop fretting."

"Off you all go, then," Percy said, shooing everyone out of the conservatory. "When you find Master Eric, give a shout and we'll meet back here to continue the festivities."

The assembled guests scattered throughout the house, including Madame Serafina, who made her way toward the library.

Decker retrieved his coat from a closet near the stairs and hurried to the front door with Daisy at his side. When he opened it, a blast of frigid winter air whistled into the entrance hall.

He looked at Daisy. "Ready to do this?"

She nodded.

Then they stepped out into the frozen, white landscape.

Nineteen

AS DAISY and Decker stepped out from under the manor house's porte-cochère, the snow crunched under their feet. The strange footprints that had been left the previous night were gone now, covered by a fresh layer of snow. The first thing that struck Decker was the lack of any other footprints except for their own. No new snow had fallen since dawn, which led him to believe that Eric had not left the house. Regardless, he decided it would be prudent to make sure and set off parallel to the building, letting his gaze roam over the landscape ahead all the way to a line of trees that marked the edge of woodlands that circled the property.

Daisy kept pace beside him; her movements clumsy in the deep snow that came up almost to her knees at times.

"I think we should talk about what we saw last night," she said in a breathy voice. "That boy who visited the children in their room is real, isn't he?"

"I'm beginning to suspect as much," Decker admitted. "Although most of the other guests don't appear to be aware of his presence. Apart from the children, only me and you have seen him."

"Lucky us." Daisy shielded her eyes against the sun, which hung low on the horizon surrounded by a pale blue winter sky without a hint of the clouds that had brought a blizzard down upon them. She squinted and looked out over the freshly fallen snow. "Have you ever seen a ghost before?"

"I have," Decker replied. He had seen many other things, too, but he kept quiet about those. "Not very long ago, in fact."

"What do you think this one wants?"

"Until we know why it's appearing to us, that's a hard question to answer. Maybe Lord Percy's renovations disturbed the ghost, and he's angry."

"That doesn't make sense. Why would a ghost be angry that the house it haunts is being maintained? After all, if the place falls down, the ghost has nowhere to live."

Decker shrugged. "Beats me. I'm just speculating. Maybe it's antisocial and doesn't like all these people being around."

"Then why would it want to play with Eric and his sister?"

"I suspect that when we find Eric, we'll get our answer," Decker said. They reached the corner of the building and turned to go down the side. Decker figured there was probably a path somewhere under the snow, but it would be impossible to find. For all he knew, they were trudging through flowerbeds. He glanced sideways at Daisy. "What about you?"

"What about me?"

"How many ghosts have you seen?"

"A few. I'm pretty sure my dormitory at the boarding school is haunted. Of course, there are always ghost stories about places like that. Most of them are probably made up by the older pupils to scare the younger kids. But there are times when I can feel a presence there. I saw it once, too. I woke up to see a black shape gliding down the middle of the hall before it vanished into the wall. I tried to convince myself that I was just dreaming, but I don't think I was. I guess I'm what some people would call gifted that way."

"Do your parents know?" Decker asked although he suspected they didn't.

Daisy shook her head. "No. They already sent me away to boarding school. If I tell them I can see ghosts, they would probably send me to a lunatic asylum instead."

"I doubt they would do that," Decker replied. He wondered what Finch would say if he knew his daughter was sensitive to the spirit world. Someone like that would be useful to the Order of St. George, but he couldn't imagine Finch would ever allow his daughter within a mile of the place. After all, not even his wife knew what Finch actually did for work. For all she knew, he was a dull civil servant shuffling papers all day and discussing governmental policy. "But maybe that should stay between you and me."

Daisy smiled. "Probably for the best." She pushed her hands into the pockets of her coat. "It is weird, though. Madame Serafina is supposed to be a spirit medium, yet she doesn't appear to have noticed anything out of the ordinary."

"I don't think Madame Serafina is all that she claims to be." They were making their way around the back of the house now and had still seen no sign that Eric had gone outside. "Her séance was nothing but cheap parlor tricks and bad acting."

"The other guests seemed to be fooled by it," Daisy said, then caught herself. "I mean..."

"Relax. You already told me that you snuck down while the séance was going on," Decker said. "And yes, most of the other guests did seem enthralled by Madame Serafina. Especially Eden. She was gripping my hand so tight at the table that I thought she might break my fingers."

Daisy laughed at that. She looked around. "I don't think we're going to find anything here, do you, Mr. Decker?"

"I don't. Wherever Eric is hiding, it isn't outside." Decker led Daisy back to the front of the house. "Please, call me John."

"I don't think my parents would approve of that."

"Well, they're not here." Decker nodded toward the chapel a couple of hundred feet away near the driveway. "Let's take a peek inside there, just to be sure, and then head back inside."

"All right... John."

"See, that wasn't so hard." They trudged through the deep snow to the chapel. The doors were closed but not locked. Decker held the door open for Daisy and then followed her inside. The chapel comprised only one room, with a small altar at one end, and five benches. Enough space for an extended family to worship in private. The walls and floor were constructed of stone. Wooden beams held a vaulted ceiling aloft. To their right, a narrow stone staircase descended underneath the chapel. Decker guessed it must lead to a crypt. He wondered how many previous owners of the manor were spending their eternity resting down there in the darkness.

Daisy shuddered. "I know I shouldn't say this in a chapel, but this place gives me the creeps."

"Me too," said Decker. He turned back toward the door. "How about we get out of here."

Twenty

AFTER AN HOUR of searching the house and grounds, they had not found Eric. Now, everyone had gathered in the drawing room where Davies had kindled a fire in the hearth.

"He simply must be in the house," Lord Percy said, standing near the fireplace with his arms folded. He looked in Decker's direction. "We know he didn't go outside because we would have seen his footprints in the snow."

"There was no sign of him on the grounds," Decker confirmed. "We also searched the chapel, but as we expected, he wasn't there either."

"This is ridiculous." Florence Lark was close to tears. "How could he just vanish?"

Her husband paced back and forth, tapping his hands absently against the sides of his legs. "We have to fetch the police. They'll know what to do."

"We can't fetch the police," Percy said, glancing toward the window. "The snow is two feet deep. We'll never get down the driveway, let alone all the way into town. It's at least three miles."

"Well, we can't just stand here doing nothing, man," Lark

snapped. "What about a telephone? You must have one of those."

"In our home back in the city, yes, we have a telephone. But not here. We're too far from the nearest exchange and it's so rural that it would be prohibitive to install."

"I'll walk to town, then," Lark said. "And bring the constable back here myself. Yes, that's what I'll do." He started toward the door.

"Don't be so foolish." Percy stepped in his path. "You'd freeze to death before you got halfway there."

"And even if you made it to town," said Lady Elizabeth," you would have a hard time convincing the constable to come here on foot. The solution is simple. We must search again and find Eric."

"We've looked everywhere." Florence stifled a sob. She was beside herself and holding her composure by the thinnest of threads. "All the bedchambers. The third-floor servant's quarters. The cellars. There is nowhere left to look. He's simply gone." With these last three words, her voice rose to a near-hysterical pitch.

A trepidatious murmur rippled through the rest of the group, including the butler, Davies, and the two maids who had abandoned their regular duties to help with the crisis. Decker could sense a subtle panic lying just beneath the surface.

"Ladies and gentlemen, that's quite enough," Percy said. "Unrestrained emotion will get us nowhere. Let's look at the facts, shall we?"

"The fact is that my son is missing and we're all just standing around here gabbing about it," Florence exclaimed, throwing her arms in the air.

"Now, darling, let the man speak." Lark went to his wife and put an arm around her.

Lord Percy nodded his appreciation, then continued. "Look,

we know the boy didn't leave the house. We also know he was here this morning before he and his sister went off to play."

"We went upstairs to the bedroom because Eric wanted to play Pirate and Traveler," said Celia, who had been sitting quietly on one of the sofas until now, with her legs drawn up underneath her and her head bent low.

"Exactly." Percy motioned toward the girl. "Like she said, they were upstairs playing a board game and grew tired of it. That's when they decided to play hide and seek—"

"We didn't grow bored with the game." Celia leaped to her feet, interrupting. "That isn't what happened. I told you already, the boy came into our room and asked us to play with him. I didn't want to do it, but Eric said it would be okay."

"Whatever. They went and hid with this imaginary boy—"

"And that's the last anyone saw of Eric." Now it was Florence's turn to interrupt. "We already know this. What's the point in going over it again? It doesn't solve anything."

"Because we might have missed a detail somewhere," Percy replied, not bothering to hide his frustration. "For goodness' sake, there has to be a rational explanation for this."

"The boy isn't imaginary." Celia stomped her foot. "Why does no one believe me?"

Eden turned to the little girl and kneeled next to her. "I believe you, honey. Does the boy have a name?"

Celia thought about this, then shook her head. "He didn't tell us his name."

"Can you tell us what the boy looked like?" Eden asked. "How about that?"

"He was just a boy."

"What was he wearing?"

"A sort of nightshirt that looked like a dress. It came all the way down to his ankles. I thought it was a funny thing for a boy his age to be wearing."

"This is ridiculous. Focusing on this phantom boy is a waste of time," Lark said. "Celia's doing nothing but regurgitating the story Lizzie told us at dinner last night."

"Hush," Eden said, looking up at Lark with a stern glare. She turned her attention back to the girl. "Where did you go with the boy?"

"We came downstairs. He said there were better places to hide down here. He told Eric that they should hide first because he knew of a hidey-hole where I would never find them."

"This really is just like that story you told us last night, Lizzie," Stour said. He was standing by the window with his arms behind his back. "A young boy going missing on Christmas Eve. Maybe the ghost of that poor unfortunate soul lured Eric away."

"That's quite enough." Lark glared at the businessman. "The situation is bad enough without you filling our heads with the idea that a ghost is responsible for this."

"No. Maybe he's right." A look of desperate hope replaced the anguish on Florence's face. "If it was the ghost, then all we need to do is ask him where he took Eric."

Lark rolled his eyes. "And how do you propose we do that, my darling?"

"Easy." Florence turned toward a wingback chair in the corner of the room, upon which sat Madame Serafina, who had remained quiet until now. "We have our very own spirit medium."

Twenty-One

MADAME SERAFINA'S head snapped up with a look something akin to that of a deer caught on the open road in front of a speeding carriage. "You want me to do what?"

"Talk to the ghost," Florence said. "Find our boy and bring him back to us."

"I can't... It's not like..." Madame Serafina stammered. "I mean, what you're asking is not so simple."

"Please?" Florence begged. She wiped a tear from her cheek. "Help us."

"I wish I could but it's not possible." Madame Serafina shook her head. "No. Simply can't be done. The veil between our world and the afterlife is not some curtain that can be swished back on demand."

Edward Lark took a step toward the medium. "Now look here, you were levitating candelabras and summoning spirits left right and center last night at the séance. Now you're telling us it's impossible to talk to a ghost that's already haunting the manor. Unless, of course, ghosts don't exist and you're nothing but a charlatan."

Madame Serafina jumped to her feet. "How dare you call me a fraud! I've been on the spiritual circuit for nigh on thirty years and no one has ever accused me of being a charlatan. Just because I can't summon a particular spirit on demand does not mean my gift is false. This is truly outrageous."

"Please, Madame Serafina, calm yourself," Lady Elizabeth said, stepping between the pair. "I'm sure that Edward is just upset. His son is missing, after all. No one here is saying you don't have a remarkable gift, but let's be honest, we employed a few... ah... dramatic effects in your performance last night."

"What's she talking about?" Lark asked, raising an eyebrow.

Madam Serafina looked sheepish. "The ectoplasm was nothing more than a ribbon of thin gauze hidden beneath my dress and pulled out to simulate spiritual energy."

"Is that so." Archibald Stour shook his head. "And the rest of the supposedly supernatural events?"

Lady Elizabeth hesitated, then said, "The candelabra. We used a silk fishing line run over a hook in the ceiling to make it look like the candelabra was floating. The window was cracked open an inch or two and Davies was standing outside pulling on it."

"I knew it," Lark bellowed. "That's why it was so darned cold in the library, too. The woman is a fraud!"

"And I suspect, why there were footprints leading up to the front door." Fitzmorris put his hands on his hips.

"No. That was nothing to do with Davies," Lady Elizabeth said. "He used the conservatory entrance to go outside and was never at the front of the house. I asked him about it this morning. Whoever made those footprints was not our butler."

"And anyway, they started in the middle of the driveway and led up to the front door, not away from it," Eden pointed out. "Unless the butler could jump an incredibly long distance, it was clearly not him."

"A fair point," Fitzmorris conceded. He jerked a thumb at Madame Serafina. "But it doesn't alter the fact that this woman is nothing but a mountebank."

"A common trickster," added Lark. "Deceiving us in such a way. It's disgraceful."

"If I did, it was only to provide a memorable experience," Madame Serafina wailed. "That is what Lady Elizabeth paid me to do."

"Doesn't make it right." Stour frowned. He looked at Lark. "I agree with you. It's shameful."

Lady Elizabeth clapped her hands. "Would everyone please calm down? Madame Serafina enhanced her séance at my request. She told me exactly what she was, and was not, capable of doing and I asked that she provide a more theatrical experience for my dinner guests, to which she agreed."

"Most of my high society clients don't want a genuine séance," said lady Serafina, recovering her composure. "They want a visceral encounter with the supernatural that will leave their party guests speechless, and they don't care if it's real."

"Well, I for one have never felt like such a fool," Stour said. "To think I actually believed that—"

Florence whirled around. Her cheeks were streaked with tears, and her face was ashen. "Would you all just shut up. I mean it. Shut up. Shut up. Shut up. My son is missing, and you are bickering about whether a floating candelabra was real or not. I don't care about any of that. I want my Eric back, and if this woman has even a modicum of talent for communicating with the dead, she might be our only hope of finding him. If you want to be outraged that Lady Elizabeth tried to provide you with a memorable Christmas, then do it later."

"Sorry," Stour mumbled, his gaze dropping to the floor.

"Yes. Me too." Fitzmorris shuffled his feet uncomfortably.

"You're right. Eric is the priority, not putting Madame Serafina's talents on trial."

Florence accepted their apologies with a curt nod, then turned back to Madame Serafina. "Now that we have put that unpleasantness behind us, I beg you to reconsider and help us find our boy."

Madame Serafina clasped her hands together. "What you are asking is no small feat. It is one thing to peek beyond the veil and see if a wandering soul wishes to communicate. It is quite another to target a specific spiritual energy. We don't even know if the ghostly boy is real, let alone willing and able to talk with us."

Daisy looked at Decker, then she stepped forward. "The boy is real. Both Mr. Decker and I have seen him."

"Daisy?" Lily stared at her daughter, a look of shock passing across her face. "What do you mean, you've seen him?"

"I saw the apparition twice last night. Once while the séance was taking place, and again later. Mr. Decker saw the ghost, too. He was following it and we bumped into each other."

"John?" Finch asked, turning his attention to Decker. "Is this true?"

Decker had not wanted to air his suspicions in front of the entire group. He had planned to pull Finch aside when the opportunity arose and discuss the situation. Now Daisy had forced his hand. "Yes. The ghost is real, unless my eyes and ears are deceiving me, which I don't believe to be the case."

Decker's statement was followed by several horrified gasps.

Eden put a hand to her forehead as if she were about to swoon. "I knew it."

Percy's attention swiveled to Decker. "Perhaps you would care to elaborate, my good man. I'm sure we are all eager to hear what you have to say on the matter."

"It's just as Daisy said. The ghost woke me in the early hours of the morning and led me downstairs. At first, I believed myself to be experiencing a lucid dream brought on by the strange surroundings and Lady Elizabeth's tales, but that was not the case, as Daisy's own experience proves."

"Then it's settled," Florence said. "Madame Serafina will hold another séance and find out why the ghost took Eric. Then we can get him back."

"No." Madame Serafina shook her head vigorously. "I won't do it. I'm sorry, but I simply won't."

"But why not?" Florence wailed, the tears flowing anew. "Tell me why you won't do it?"

Madame Serafina drew in a long and trembling breath. Her shoulders slumped. "Because I can't."

Twenty-Two

"I THINK you had better explain yourself, right now," Edward Lark said. "Your claims of mediumship change with each telling, and now you can't do anything at all, or so you say. You're upsetting my wife, and I simply won't stand for it."

"I wasn't lying about having a gift," Lady Serafina replied in a small voice. "But it can't be used the way you want. I don't see spirits or converse with them. I sense them and sometimes get vague impressions of their intentions. When I was a child, I could see the ghosts of those who had passed on, but as I grew into adulthood, I lost that ability. It faded."

"Well, that's jolly convenient," Fitzmorris said. "The woman claims she can sense ghosts but can't actually figure out what they want or why they're hanging around. If you ask me, it's all just another excuse to hide the fact that she's a fake."

This time, Madame Serafina did not argue. She sat back down in the chair and placed her hands on her lap. "Think what you will. I am under no obligation to defend myself to anyone, and I certainly never said I could rescue missing children."

Decker had remained quiet during this exchange, deep in

thought, but now he spoke up. "Hounding this poor woman is getting us nowhere except to provide an easy scapegoat. I think it's time we tried a different approach."

"If you have any suggestions, now would be the time to voice them," Percy said.

Decker stepped into the middle of the room. "As we have already established, there appears to be a ghost haunting this house. That ghost has led a young boy away for unknown reasons. If we are to find Eric, we must get to the bottom of what the ghost is doing here, and who he is. Only then will we understand his motivations and hopefully reunite Eric with his parents."

"How in blazes are we supposed to do any of that?" Fitzmorris asked. "The one person who claims she can talk to ghosts isn't willing to even give it a try."

Decker turned to Lord Percy. "Apart from what you've already told us, how much of the history of this house do you know?"

"Not much at all," Percy said. "It was owned by the Blackthorn family before us. They built it. But like I said, Alistair despised the place. He never really talked much about it, even after I agreed to purchase it from him. He's the last of the Blackthorn line and I sometimes wonder if this house reminds him of all his family have lost over the centuries."

"They haven't lost that much, my dear," Lady Elizabeth said. "He's filthy rich and sits alongside you in the Lords."

"Granted." Lord Percy lapsed into silence.

Decker took the opportunity to steer the conversation back to more important matters. "There were no documents that came with the house detailing its history?"

"If there were, they would be in the library, I suppose," Percy replied.

"You didn't bring the books with you?"

"Yes, well, some of them. The majority were already here when we bought the place. I haven't even really looked at them, to tell the truth. I have little interest in reading antique books, but they lend the place an air of gravitas."

"What are you thinking?" asked Finch.

"If the books in that library came with the house, there might be journals and other documentation that will shed light on its history," Decker said.

"You think we might be able to confirm if the story about the boy going missing a hundred years ago is true?" Finch rubbed his chin.

"Exactly. I don't believe it's a coincidence that lady Elizabeth told us a story about a boy vanishing a century ago in this very house on Christmas Eve, and the same thing repeats today. If we can confirm that story, we will be one step closer to understanding the haunting and Eric's disappearance."

"I still find it hard to believe that this house is actually haunted," Lark said. "You're asking us to take an incredible leap of faith."

"Do you want your son back, or not?" Decker asked in an even voice.

"Why yes. That goes without saying."

"Then you might wish to keep an open mind. As you are well aware, we have already searched the building from top to bottom, as well as the grounds. Eric does not appear to be on the premises, which is impossible, considering we know he didn't leave the house. With no other explanation presenting itself, a supernatural one should at least be considered."

"Especially since there is a real ghost here," Daisy said. "I saw it and don't care what anyone else believes."

"Daisy—" Lily reached out to her daughter.

"I'm serious, mother. The ghost visited me, and I refuse to be quiet about it."

"I don't know," Lark said. "You want us to waste valuable time searching through a bunch of moldy old books just to see if some old wife's tale about the house might be true instead of continuing our search for Eric? I really don't think I can go along with that plan."

"You can, and you will, Edward." Eden turned to her husband with an expression of determination. "As Mr. Decker has already pointed out, we have searched the house, to no avail. Doing so again will not change that outcome. It's a pointless endeavor. Finding out more about this phantom boy that led our son away is not." She turned to Decker. "If you think that searching the library will bring us one step closer to getting Eric back, I'm willing to give it a go and Edward will be more than happy to help, won't you, dear?"

"I think it's a foolish distraction, and nothing more," Lark said. "But I'm willing to admit that searching the house did not yield any results. I'll give it an hour, and no longer. After that, I'm resuming my search."

"Fair enough." Decker shrugged. "In the meantime, I suggest we all go next door to the library and see what we can find."

"I'll stay here with Celia," Eden said. "Maybe she will remember something else that will help us."

"Good idea." Decker stepped out into the entrance hall and turned toward the library.

Everyone else filed out behind him, except for Madame Serafina who lingered in her chair for a moment, then grumbled under her breath and stood up, following along behind.

Twenty-Three

"THERE ARE a lot of books in here," Fitzmorris said, standing in the library doorway and looking around at the bookshelves lining the walls with a dismayed look on his face. "There must be thousands of volumes. How will we ever find what we're looking for?"

"There are eleven of us," Decker said. "If we each take a couple of bookcases, we will be through this in no time."

"I admire your optimism, old boy," Percy said. A few minutes before, he had dismissed Davies and the pair of maids and told them to resume their normal duties, at least for the time being. Now he looked unsure of himself. "Perhaps I should not have sent the staff away so quickly. I have a good mind to call them back."

"No need for that," said Decker. "I'm sure the task isn't as bad as it looks. The majority of these books will probably be fiction and easily discounted."

"Either way, we had better get to work." Percy headed toward a bookcase and began perusing the volumes lining the shelves.

One by one, the others followed suit.

Decker retreated to the rear of the room, where a library ladder stood leaning against the shelves. He pushed it to one side and began studying the books, most of which turned out to be nonfiction titles related to science and the arts. They looked old. The spines were brittle and cracked. When he pulled them out, plumes of dust erupted into the air making me wonder how long it had been since anyone had looked at any of these volumes. He moved from the bottom shelves up toward the top, using the ladder to reach the uppermost books, but found nothing of interest. After descending the ladder and moving it further along, he started again on the next set of shelves.

After a while, Daisy approached and lingered at his rear. "I think my mother is upset with me."

"Because you admitted to seeing a ghost?"

Daisy nodded. "She's weirdly over-protective. Sometimes I feel like she finds dealing with me to be a chore. I think I embarrass her."

"I can't imagine that's true." Decker replaced another heavy volume and turned toward the young woman. "I'm sure both your parents love you with all their hearts."

"Then why did she send me away to boarding school?"

"Perhaps she wanted you to receive a quality education," Decker replied.

"There are plenty of schools in London that I could have attended. Sometimes I feel like it's a case of out of sight, out of mind."

"I think this is a conversation you should have with her," Decker said, feeling uncomfortable inserting himself into the family affairs of Finch and his daughter.

Daisy glanced over her shoulder. Lily was on the other side of the room, pulling books off the shelves and giving each a cursory examination before putting them back. She paid her daughter no heed. "Believe me, I've tried more than once. Honestly, I think she will be relieved when I turn eighteen and am no longer beholden to her."

"That is something I'm not qualified to comment on," Decker said. He motioned to the next bookcase. "You want to lend a hand?"

"Sure." Daisy walked over to the bookcase and kneeled, examining the books on the lower shelves. She looked up at Decker. "Sorry, I don't mean to burden you with my troubles."

"Don't worry about it." Decker climbed the ladder again to examine the uppermost shelves.

Daisy climbed to her feet. "It's just that sometimes, I feel like I don't really fit in—like I'm an interloper pretending to be someone I'm not. Does that make sense?"

"I think all teenagers feel like that at one point or another," Decker said tactfully. "Give it time, and you'll see it's not the case."

"Easy for you to say." Daisy withdrew another book, then let out a small squeal and almost dropped it when a silverfish scuttled along the binding toward her fingers. She pushed the book back in place and pulled a face. "Yuck. Disgusting. When was the last time anyone took any of these books off the shelf?"

"It's just a silverfish," said Decker.

"I hate bugs." Daisy shuddered. "How much longer do we have to do this?"

"Until we've either searched the entire library or found what we're looking for," Decker replied. "There must be something about the history of the house somewhere in this room."

"And if we don't find what we're looking for?" Daisy ran her finger along the spines of several books. She paused at a volume that had no writing on the spine, removed it, examined it briefly, and slipped it back in among the others. "What do we do then?"

"We think of something else," Decker said. The library was a long shot. Even though the books had come with the house, that didn't mean that they had been there for any great length of time. For all Decker knew, the previous owners might have brought the books in as décor and couldn't be bothered to take them when they left. He doubted if Percy would know, either. But he suspected that wasn't true. Even to Decker's untrained eye, many of the volumes looked like antiques, although he guessed they were not particularly valuable. After all, no one would leave a small fortune in antique books behind if they could sell them and make money.

He moved the ladder again and was about to climb back up to the higher shelves when there was an exclamation of excitement from across the room.

Lily was holding a large thick volume bound in rich brown leather. She held it up with a visible effort. "I think this might be important. The pages are handwritten. It looks like a diary. And it's old."

Decker exchanged a glance with Daisy.

She grinned. "You were right. There is something here."

"We shall see," Decker said, but deep down, he knew they had found what they were looking for.

Twenty-Four

EVERYONE GATHERED AROUND THE BOOK, which Lily had placed on a reading table in the middle of the room. It must have been well over a hundred years old. The bindings were cracked, and they had been repaired at some point. The leather was scratched and mottled with age. There were no markings on the front cover or spine to identify what lay within, but when Decker opened the antique tome, he found a hand-written title plate.

A journal of Blackthorn Manor
1557–1856
Written by Lady Edwina Margaret Blackthorn
compiled from accounts by my ancestors,
family, and my own recollection

Decker felt a surge of excitement. "The answers we seek may lie within these pages."

"Well, get on with it then old boy," Percy said. "Let's see what we have."

Decker turned the title page gently and came to an annotation written in the same flowing hand.

The history of Blackthorn Manor, as recounted within these pages, was passed down to me in oral and written form by my family, both living and dead. It has been a project of love spanning many decades but sadly, my eyesight is no longer of sufficient quality to continue. It is my fervent hope that in the coming years another family member may step up to the mantle, for there are many pages left to be written, but if not, this is as complete a chronicle as I can make using both my knowledge of family history, and the assorted papers, letters, and records that my ancestors have preserved through the ages.

Edwina, June 1866

"I can't believe this has been in our library since we bought the place and we were unaware of its existence," Lady Elizabeth said. "It's absolutely astonishing."

"And quite a feat that it survived intact," Percy added.

"I don't wish to be a bore, but we can marvel at our good fortune in discovering this volume another time," Fitzmorris said. "Right now, we need to find out if anything within these pages will give us a clue regarding Eric's disappearance."

"Of course." Lady Elizabeth glanced toward Florence. "Please forgive my excitement."

"If these pages lead us to Eric, I will join you in that excitement." Florence fought back a sob and turned away briefly to wipe her eyes.

Decker turned the page again, careful not to damage the fragile document. The next leaf was blank. The one after that contained a heading that read:

The earliest days of
Blackthorn Manor.

Decker skimmed the text below, which detailed the Manor's construction in 1524, and the earliest years of its use. There was nothing of any significance over the next several pages until he came to another heading that caught his eye, mostly because of something Lady Elizabeth had mentioned during dinner the previous night.

"When you were telling ghost stories last night at dinner, you mentioned the ghost of a priest," Decker said, glancing her way. "Is that part of the folklore surrounding this house, or did you make it up to entertain us?"

"I can't speak to its validity regarding a real haunting," Lady Elizabeth replied. "But the story is genuine. It was told to me by a lady in the local Women's Guild. They meet once a month in town and asked me to come along last month when we came up from the city since I was new to the area."

"And where did this woman hear the tale?" Stour asked.

"I suppose it is local knowledge," Lady Elizabeth replied, a hint of annoyance in her voice. "But she also mentioned a trove of documents taken from the house many years ago by the local historical society to prevent their deterioration."

"Maybe even the very documents that were used to write that book," Finch said, looking down at the leather-bound volume.

"Possibly." Lady Elizabeth nodded thoughtfully. "I have been meaning to visit the historical society and read the documents but have not yet found the time."

"This is all very fascinating, but I would like to hear what Mr. Decker has found in that book," Fitzmorris said.

"Of course." Lady Elizabeth motioned toward Decker. "Please, continue."

Decker cleared his throat. "I stopped at the following passage because it may provide a clue regarding Eric's disappearance."

"Well, what does it say?" Percy asked, impatiently.

"If you give me a moment to read it, I'll let you know," Decker said, turning his attention back to the book and reading aloud.

> The following account was written by my ancestor, Oliver, son of the man who built Blackthorn Manor, in a secret letter to his sweetheart, Isabel, who had fled England for the continent to escape religious persecution. I transcribe the relevant sections here to preserve them for history.
>
> -October 23, 1588
>
> Last night, the troubles that have plagued this fair land found their way to our door. As you know, my sweet Isabel, my family has been concerned by recent decrees handed down by Queen Elizabeth outlawing our faith and making the practicing of such faith hazardous to the extreme. Yet we felt it was our Christian duty to fight back against that tyranny in our own small way. To

that end, we have been sheltering a priest for the last three months.

Father Vincent Callahan will eventually make his way to Ireland, but the route there has become dangerous of late, and he was forced to seek refuge among friends. We had hoped to disguise him as a distant family member down on his luck, but our visiting 'uncle' must have raised the suspicions of someone hereabouts. Late yesterday evening, pursuivants searched our home. These priest hunters, full of self-righteous fervor, conducted a most thorough ransacking of Blackthorn Manor but were unsuccessful in their endeavors thanks to certain hidden spaces my father had the forethought to include when constructing the manor. Those secret chambers saved Father Callahan's life, but we might not be so lucky the next time. The priest hunters are catching on to such hiding places and becoming better at finding them. If that happens, we may all end up hung, drawn, and quartered.

Decker stopped reading. There was more, lots of it, but he had made his point.

Several seconds passed in silence before Daisy spoke up. "What do you think the person who wrote this letter meant when they said there were secret chambers in the house?"

"He meant priest holes," Percy said. "Hidden rooms and

spaces where clergymen could hide from the authorities. Sometimes they were forced to stay in them for so long that they either starved or suffocated to death. A lot of manor houses from the Elizabethan era had them."

"Including this one, apparently," Stour said.

"It doesn't surprise me, although I have found no evidence of priest holes during our renovation."

"That doesn't mean they aren't here," lady Elizabeth said. "Priest holes were notoriously well concealed for obvious reasons. The Elizabethan priest hunters were ruthless in their pursuit and cruel in the execution of their task. Neither the priest in hiding, nor those assisting him, would want to risk discovery."

"But how does this help us?" Fitzmorris asked.

"It could explain why we can't find Eric," Decker said. "He might have discovered the entrance to one of these hidden chambers and become trapped on the other side, unable to free himself."

"Mercy." Florence raised her hands to her mouth in despair. She looked at Percy. "You said priests sometimes suffocated in such places."

"They did," Percy replied. "The priest holes were often airtight because otherwise, the authorities could find them by using candles to search for drafts of air escaping from within."

"But that means..." Florence's voice trailed off.

"If we don't find Eric soon, he might not survive," Decker said.

Twenty-Five

"YOU REALLY THINK Eric is in that much danger?" Fitzmorris asked Decker.

"I do," Decker replied. "I also suspect that it's not the first time this has happened."

"The boy who went missing a hundred years ago."

"Yes. The coincidence is too great to ignore, given the facts." Decker was leafing through the book now. "I suspect we will find proof of the boy's existence somewhere in these pages." Near the back of the book, he stopped and read silently for a minute before looking up. "This is it."

"Well, what does it say?" Percy asked, leaning to peer over Decker's shoulder. "Don't leave us all on tenterhooks."

"Yes, read it to us." Fitzmorris folded his arms and waited.

"Very well." Decker skimmed the passage silently one more time to digest it. The entry was written in the same flowing handwriting as the front of the book, except that now the letterforms were not so neat, as if the person who authored it was battling a tremor in their hand. Decker wondered if it was from age or

103

emotion. Perhaps both. The subject matter was certainly more personal. He cleared his throat and began to read.

This is, I must confess, the hardest part of this journal for me to write because it involves one of the saddest moments in my own life. An event I have put off committing to paper for many years. But now, as I near the end of my endeavor, I can no longer prevaricate. I must recount the dreadful incident that brought my father to drink and my mother to an early grave. I refer, of course, to my younger brother, Ambrose, who vanished without a trace on Christmas Eve, in the year of our Lord, 1811.

Even now, I remember the events that occurred that Christmas eve as if it were yesterday. It was a wintry day, with a fall of snow surrounding Blackthorn Manor like a white shroud. Father came home from town in the morning with a goose bigger than any I had ever seen and made a great show of handing it over to the kitchen staff to pluck.

The smells of baking were redolent in the house as all sorts of delicious pastries and sweet treats were prepared for the next day, although my favorite was always plum pudding. There would be fresh crusty bread, too, cooked on the great hearth in the kitchen.

We played games all afternoon. I beat my father three times at draughts, while Ambrose allowed my mother to win dominoes in a very gentlemanly fashion, and my sister Jane was reading a book by the hearth. In the early evening, we gathered in the drawing room to open presents, and as usual, father invited the servants to join us and make sure that each of them received a present from every member of the household. This was an important tradition in our family and a way of showing gratitude for their hard work in keeping Blackthorn Manor running all year long. It was only then that we were allowed to open our own presents.

Decker stopped to catch his breath.

Daisy furrowed her brow. "Why were they opening their presents on the night of Christmas Eve?"

"Because it was the tradition back then," Percy said. "They didn't have Christmas trees either. It was a mostly German tradition until Queen Victoria popularized it in the middle of the nineteenth century."

"We're getting off subject and we don't have time to waste," Lady Elizabeth said, exasperated. She motioned to Decker. "Please continue reading."

Decker turned his attention back to the Journal.

After the presents had been opened, and the grandfather clock in the grand entrance hall struck nine, we were sent to bed. Ambrose was most excited and protested all the way to his bed-chamber, but mother was unrelenting and the three of us were soon tucked up in bed. My own excitement at the day's events, while not as great as my brother's, prevented me from sleeping until the rest of the household retired two hours later.

It was after that, I presume, that my brother snuck from his bed and unwittingly set in motion the chain of events that would take him from us. To this day, I cannot say with any accuracy what occurred in those early hours while everyone else was sleeping, but I do remember waking briefly at the sound of a door opening and closing in the hallway beyond my room followed by soft footsteps. I woke Jane and we peeked out into the hallway but saw nothing amiss and so went back to bed. I lay awake for a while after that, wondering about the footsteps but afraid to investigate lest my parents catch me. Eventually, I drifted back to sleep.

The next morning—Christmas morning—we rose to find Ambrose missing from his bed and no sign of him anywhere in the house. The only clue regarding his disappearance was a cup and ball game he had received the evening before. It was lying on the floor in the drawing room, which was not where it had been left. The ball, which was usually attached to the cup by a piece of string, had detached and rolled away, coming to rest near the fireplace. All we could think was that he had snuck back down to play with it again. What happened after that, no one could say, except that he never went back to bed.

My parents were beside themselves, naturally, and a search was mounted, which yielded no results. For the next week, searches were a regular occurrence, and my father even went into the woods to see if Ambrose might have wandered outside and become lost there. No one really believed that my brother had left the house, though. The ground was still covered with snow and there were no footprints anywhere to be found other than those of the searchers. In the end, my parents admitted defeat and slowly realized that their son was lost forever, although how and why, no one would ever find out.

Decker stopped reading. He closed the book and stood, then turned to the group. "I think that is proof enough that the story of a young boy vanishing on Christmas Eve a hundred years ago is true. His name was Ambrose, and I suspect it is his ghost that has been plaguing us."

"And leading my Eric away to die in some hidden chamber," Florence said, sniffing.

"Calm yourself, my dear," Lark said. "We don't know that is what happened."

"Yes, we do." Celia was standing in the doorway, with Eden lingering close behind.

"I'm sorry. She jumped up and ran in here before I could stop her," Eden said. "She wanted to see what was happening."

"It's quite all right," Percy said. He looked at Celia. "Why don't you go back into the drawing room and let the adults handle this."

"No." Celia stomped her foot. "I know what happened to Eric. The ghost boy promised to show him a hidey-hole. A place where I would never find them. That's where my brother went. He's in the hidey-hole with the ghost, and I don't think he's ever coming back."

Twenty-Six

"THE PRIEST HOLE COULD BE ANYWHERE," Florence exclaimed in a panic.

They were gathered in the grand entrance hall. It was dark outside. Over the last few hours, the clouds had returned, and the snow was falling again thick and fast, as if to punctuate the fact that they were well and truly on their own.

"That's not strictly correct," Finch said. "We know it's not in the conservatory, partly because three-quarters of the walls are glass, and also because we were all gathered there when Eric went missing."

"We also know it's unlikely to be upstairs," Decker chimed in. "The ghost led Eric and Celia to the ground floor, which increases the likelihood that the priest hole is on this level."

"There might be a priest hole on each floor." Percy stood with his hands pushed deep into his pockets. "After all, if the Queen's soldiers came knocking, you would want to hide from them as quickly as possible. You certainly wouldn't want to be running up and down stairs while they were waiting at your door."

"A fair point," Finch conceded. "But as John said, the ghost brought the children down here, so it stands to reason that this is where we should look."

"I can vouch that Eric didn't enter the kitchens," said a new voice from behind the group. It was Davies, whose light-footed approach had gone unnoticed until he spoke. "Either myself, the cook, or one or other of the maids were present in the kitchens at all times until the alarm was raised."

"That's a fair point," Percy said. "Thank you, Davies."

"You're welcome." Davies bowed a little. "Unless you have more urgent duties for me to perform, I would like to participate in the search. I have spent more time in the house than anyone else here during the last six months while making sure it was ready for habitation."

"Yes. Of course." Percy nodded. "Your help would be most appreciated."

"How are we going to find this priest hole?" asked Stour. "It must be jolly well hidden if the priest hunters couldn't find it, and they knew what to look for. We don't have an inkling."

"If only we had more information," Eden said. "I don't suppose there are plans for the house anywhere?"

"If there are, I haven't seen them," Percy replied. "Floor plans would have been gosh-darned useful during the renovation."

"I can't imagine they would have left such things lying around, especially if the priest hole was in them," Lady Elizabeth pointed out. "If there are any, they are as well-hidden as the secret chamber we are searching for."

"We are wasting time," Florence said with exasperation.

"Agreed." Decker glanced around the group. "We might as well get on with it. Remember, we are looking for a hidden chamber. I suspect the door will be so well concealed that we will not find it simply by looking for unusual seams in wall panels or knocking on walls and listening for hollow spaces within. If it were that easy, the priest hunters would have found it in short order. Instead, we should look for the mechanism that opens it."

"How the devil do you propose we do that?" Fitzmorris asked. "It's not like we're going to come across a random doorknob screwed to the wall with a sign hanging off that says 'secret room'."

"If I had the answer to that," Decker replied, "we wouldn't need to search."

Twenty-Seven

THEY SEARCHED for three hours to no avail, splitting up and taking different rooms. Decker, Finch, and Daisy searched the library, hoping to find a bookcase that swung open, or shelves that concealed a false back. They found none of these things, even after pulling, poking, and prodding every piece of molding and decorative embellishment looking for a catch or door release.

Eventually, they concluded that either there was no hidden room within the library walls, or it was so well concealed that they would never find it.

Finch slumped down into a chair, looking thoroughly defeated. "I hate to be a negative Nellie, but we could search this house for a month and not find the priest hole, assuming it even exists."

"It exists," Decker said. "It must. There is no other explanation for Eric's disappearance."

"Not to mention what the ghost said." Daisy flopped down next to her father. "He mentioned a hidey-hole Celia would never find. If that doesn't sound like a secret room, I don't know what does."

"Speaking of ghosts, you and I are going to have a little talk when all this is over."

"Father, I can't help that I'm sensitive to such things." Daisy took her father's hand. "It's perfectly all right. You don't need to worry."

"I'll be the judge of that," Finch said. "But now is not the time to discuss it."

Daisy looked up at Decker. "Do you see what I mean? They are always treating me like a child, even though I will be an adult in a few months."

"I think this is one conversation I'm going to stay out of for the moment," Decker said. "But your father is right. This isn't the time or place—and you're right. The ghost told Celia about a hidey-hole. There's a secret chamber somewhere in this house. I'm sure of it."

"Granted, it's the most logical explanation," Finch said, turning his attention to Decker once more. "But explain this. If Eric is trapped in some hidden room and can't get out, why can't we hear him hollering? He must be terrified."

"Maybe the priest hole is soundproofed," Decker said. "After all, they wouldn't want the priest hunters to hear the person concealed within."

"I would assume that if you're being hunted by murderous soldiers who want to cut you into pieces, it would be in your best interest to keep quiet, regardless."

"Any luck in here?" Said a hopeful voice from the doorway.

Decker turned to see Lord Percy standing there with William and Eden Fitzmorris at his back.

He shook his head. "No. We found nothing."

"Same here, I'm afraid," Percy said, stepping into the room. "We searched the dining room high and low but came up empty. I'm beginning to think the fates are not on our side in this."

"We can't give up," Decker said. "The Larks are counting on us to find their son."

"I'm not admitting defeat, dear boy. Far from it. But you have to admit, things don't appear to be going our way."

"Maybe someone else has had more luck," Finch said.

"I'm sure we would have heard about it if that were the case." Decker sank into a chair and folded his arms. He felt helpless. If his suspicions were correct, Eric was trapped somewhere with no way out, and they could not help him. His mind turned to the passage in the journal sitting on the table to his left. The one that detailed the disappearance of another boy a hundred years ago to the day. A boy that was never found.

It felt like history was repeating itself and they were powerless to stop it. He harbored little hope that anyone would discover the priest hole.

Over the next fifteen minutes, the rest of the group filed into the library, each with their own tale of defeat, and proved him correct.

With no hope of a resolution in sight, the mood in the library turned dark. Florence had become withdrawn and tearful. Her husband paced the room, walking back and forth with his hands in his pockets and a distant look on his face. All the while, he muttered under his breath.

Celia sat down on the couch next to Daisy and stared into the crackling fire burning in the hearth as if she thought Eric would magically appear there. When Daisy put an arm around her, the girl shrugged it off wordlessly.

An uncomfortable silence fell upon the room. No one wished to be the first to say out loud what they were all thinking--that they might find Eric too late, or not at all.

Eventually, after several minutes passed, Eden raised a tentative hand as if looking for permission to speak. She cleared her throat. "Since no one else has any new ideas, I would like to make a suggestion." She hesitated. "It's rather unusual."

"Please, feel free," Percy said in a despondent tone. "At this point, I'm willing to entertain any idea, no matter how unusual."

"I think we should hold another séance."

Madame Serafina, who was sitting in the corner and doing her best to look invisible, looked up sharply.

"We already discussed that," Stour replied. "The psychic, or whatever she is, said she can't do it."

"I know. But that doesn't mean the rest of us shouldn't give it a go. If the ghost boy is real, maybe he'll appear anyway and show us where he took Eric."

"Or maybe nothing will happen, just like last night," Fitz-morris said. "What hope do we have of summoning a spirit when the person who claims to be an expert couldn't even do it?"

"I've been thinking about that," Decker said, standing up. "I'm not so sure that Madame Serafina didn't summon a spirit during the séance last night."

"What are you talking about?" Percy asked.

"The footsteps in the snow." Decker moved closer to the fire and turned to face everyone. "At the height of the séance, the doorbell rang and when we answered, no one was there. All we saw was a set of footprints leading from the driveway up to the door. Given the thick layer of snow, no earthly person could have done that without also revealing where they went afterward."

"Madame Serafina can't have summoned the ghost of Ambrose during the séance," Daisy pointed out. "I saw him before you answered the door. He led me downstairs. I was listening to the séance when the doorbell rang."

"She might not have summoned Ambrose," Decker said. "He was probably already here. But according to Lady Elizabeth, there are many other ghost stories surrounding Blackthorne Manor. I think Madame Serafina does have genuine spiritual abilities—even if she underestimates them—and she drew one of those other spirits out of the woodwork, even if she didn't intend to."

"I still don't see how that helps us," Fitzmorris said. "The woman refuses to do anything."

Decker turned to Madame Serafina. "Then maybe we should ask her again, since willing or otherwise, she may be our only hope."

Twenty-Eight

ALL EYES TURNED to Madame Serafina.

A look of quiet resignation passed across her face. She stood up and straightened her ankle-length black dress, smoothing a wrinkle from the fabric before turning her attention to the expectant group.

"I suppose it would be wrong of me to once again refuse your request under the circumstances," she said. "But I warn you not to place all hope of finding the boy upon my performance. I know my own abilities, and I fear you will be disappointed."

"In other words, she's telling us yet again that she's nothing more than a charlatan," Lark said. He looked at Decker. "I hope you're right about this because honestly, I don't have much faith in this woman and I'm still struggling to accept that a ghost, of all things"—he shook his head in disbelief—"led my boy away and trapped him in a chamber nobody can find."

"Please, at least give her a chance," Decker said, placing a hand on Lark's shoulder. "We have explored every other avenue to find your son and have so far drawn a blank. Of course, we won't rest until Eric is safely reunited with you." He glanced toward Lark's wife. "What harm can it do to try this?"

"Mr. Decker is right," Florence said, looking at her husband. "It can do no harm to let Madame Serafina try."

Lark gave a small huff but offered no further resistance. He went to the window and stood with his back to the room, gazing out into the snow-filled night.

"Madame Serafina," Lady Elizabeth said at length. "Last night was for entertainment, but now it appears you will be performing a real séance. Is there anything we should do to prepare?"

"Nothing beyond providing a table and chairs that will allow us to link hands. That much was real. The table we used last night will be suitable."

"Very good. Is there a particular location that you would like to use?"

"The library will be fine." Madame Serafina looked around. "So long as only those partaking in the séance are present."

"In that case, I will have the table and chairs brought back and set up." She glanced toward Davies, who nodded silently and slipped from the room. "Then we can begin."

"No." Madame Serafina shook her head. "We cannot. We will have—"

"Typical," Lark interrupted, turning away from the window with a derisive snort. "The woman does nothing but change her mind. One minute she'll help us, the next she won't. I told you this was a waste of time."

Madame Serafina fixed Lark with a stony glare. "If you had let me finish, I was going to say that midnight is the best time to perform the séance, for that is when the barrier between the worlds of the living and the dead is at its thinnest."

"Midnight?" Florence wrung her hands together. "It's only nine o'clock. That's three hours away."

"I'm aware of that," replied Madame Serafina. "But if we are to have any hope of success, we must make sure the conditions are perfect. Even then, I have my doubts."

"Midnight it is," Decker said. "In the meantime, I suggest we keep ourselves busy by performing another search of the house."

"You think we'll find something now that we couldn't before?" Fitzmorris asked.

"No." Decker turned toward the door. "But sitting around here and doing nothing will only add to our frustration and make the time pass slower."

Twenty-Nine

AT MIDNIGHT, everyone gathered in the library. No candelabra sat in the middle of the table this time. The window was closed, too, and Decker was sure Madame Serafina had secreted no fake ectoplasm about her body. Unlike the previous evening's performance, there would be no shenanigans tonight.

Madame Serafina sat at the table, which was covered with a black cloth. Her hands rested in her lap, and her eyes were closed. At the sound of the library door opening, she opened them and looked up.

"Please, will everyone take a seat? It doesn't matter where so long as we can all link hands." Madame Serafina placed her hands on the table. After everyone sat down, she spoke to Davies, who lingered in the library doorway. "Would you lower the lighting and close the doors."

"Is that so you can perform more fakery under the guise of darkness?" Stour asked with a note of contempt in his voice.

"Absolutely not. I merely wish the light level lowered, not turned off completely. It will aid my concentration." She watched the butler go around the room and lower the flames on the wall sconces until the library descended into a gloomy half-light.

Davies retreated and pulled the doors closed, leaving the assembled group looking at each other across the table.

Madame Serafina offered her hands to those sitting to her left and right. "Please, everyone, take the hands of the people next to you."

Decker was sitting between Finch and Eden. He took their hands and waited to see what would happen next.

Madame Serafina waited a few moments, as if gathering her thoughts, then let out a slow and measured breath. "I will begin the séance now. Just as you did last night, please do not break the circle for any reason, even if we are successful in summoning a spirit. I would ask that you all concentrate on the subject of our séance tonight, the little boy named Ambrose, who disappeared on this same night a hundred years ago. You may keep your eyes open or close them, but please do not become distracted. Only by the combined force of our determination will we be able to draw him forth.

"If a spirit appears to us, whether it be Ambrose or otherwise, please do not interact with it. I shall converse with the spirit to find the information we desire. The séance will be less dramatic than the one we held last night. Do not expect to see or hear anything out of the ordinary until we connect with the spirit plain. Lastly, please realize that we may not be successful. Contacting the dead is no easy task, and our pleas often go unheard. Does everyone understand?"

There was a murmur of responses. A few people nodded.

Madame Serafina appeared pleased with what she heard. She took another deep breath, then lowered her head and closed her eyes. Soon, her breathing became shallow, as if she were falling into a light slumber. But she was not asleep, because her lips were moving. Decker could hear her mumbling in an almost lyrical fashion but could not make out the words.

Outside, a blizzard howled. Snow swirled against the library window. A grandfather clock sitting near the conservatory door chimed twelve times, its voice melancholy. The last peal lingered in the air, echoing through the cavernous entrance hall before fading away.

Madame Serafina lifted her head. Her eyes snapped open. She spoke in a low and husky voice. "The spirits are gathering. I can sense them all around us."

Decker felt Eden shiver. He glanced toward her, but she didn't notice. Her attention was riveted on the medium sitting across the table.

Percy coughed and mumbled a quick apology.

Madame Serafina appeared not to notice. Her eyes lifted toward the ceiling, then rolled back in her head. A small noise escaped her mouth, something between a whimper and a gasp, before her head dropped forward again.

"My goodness. Is she alright?" Eden asked.

"Quiet." Fitzmorris, who was sitting on the other side of her, gave his wife a disapproving look. "Madame Serafina said not to disturb her, no matter what happened."

"I'm sorry," Eden whispered. "But she looks like she's having a seizure."

"I'm sure this is all part of the act," Fitzmorris replied. "She was much more dramatic last night."

Lady Elizabeth leaned forward. "Hush. Both of you."

Fitzmorris opened his mouth to reply but thought better of it.

Eden was still observing Madame Serafina with a worried expression on her face. When the medium's head jerked back up, she jumped and clamped her mouth shut to avoid uttering a squeal.

"I call upon the spirit of Ambrose Blackthorn," the medium cried in a shrill voice. "Come forth, oh spirit, and speak with us. We implore you."

Florence looked around the room as if she expected the ghostly boy to materialize right there and then, but nothing happened.

Madame Serafina was not done. "Ambrose Blackthorn. If you are close, reveal yourself."

Still, nothing happened.

Decker began to think that Madame Serafina was right, and she did not possess any natural ability to contact the dead. Or maybe the ghost boy just did not wish to make an appearance.

The medium opened her eyes. She looked around the circle of expectant faces peering back at her.

"The veil is difficult to penetrate tonight," she said in a small voice. "I will try one last time, but I fear the spirits are unresponsive."

Florence gulped back a cry of anguish. Edward Lark squeezed her hand. "It's alright, my dear. It was always a long shot."

"No. It's not all right." Florence turned to him. "If this fails, we will never see our Eric again. I just know it."

"Silence. I need to concentrate." Madame Serafina closed her eyes again. She took a long and steady breath, releasing the tension from her body. "I call upon the spirit of Ambrose Blackthorn. Come to us this night."

Silence. There was no drop in temperature. The lights did not flicker. If there were any ghosts nearby, they were staying hidden.

Madame Serafina stood up and spoke in a loud, stern voice. "Ambrose Blackthorn. I command thee to appear."

This time, something happened. The words had barely left her mouth when, from the grand entrance hall beyond the library doors, there was a mighty crash.

Thirty

PERCY JUMPED TO HIS FEET, startled. "What in the devil was that?"

"I'm going take a look." Archibald Stour was already rushing toward the door.

Finch jumped up to follow.

Decker pushed his chair back and started toward the door.

Madame Serafina—apparently roused from her spiritual stupor—looked around, surprised. "Where is everyone going?"

"There was a crash out in the entrance hall," Percy said as he pulled the library doors open. "We're going to see what it was."

"But we haven't finished the séance yet," Madame Serafina said with little emotion. Decker suspected that she was secretly relieved at the interruption since they were getting nowhere summoning the young boy's spirit.

Percy stepped into the grand entrance hall with Decker and the others right behind him. The cause of the ear-splitting crash was instantly obvious. One of the oil paintings hanging in the hall--the one closest to the library that depicted Edmund and Phillipa Blackthorn, the founders of Blackthorn Manor--lay on the ground face up. The couple gazed out from beneath cracked and yellowed varnish with the same stiff expressions as when they were hanging on the wall.

"Well, I'll be," Percy said, looking at the dirty oblong outline on the wall where the picture had previously hung. "The nails are still there."

"Maybe the wire broke?" Lady Elizabeth said. "Some of these paintings are hundreds of years old and they probably haven't been moved in at least that long."

"Picked a hell of a time to jump off the wall," Stour said. "Right in the middle of a bloody séance. I almost keeled over with fright."

"Maybe we should pick it back up," Eden said. "Doesn't seem right to leave them on the floor like that."

"Right-ho." Percy rubbed his hands together. "Who wants to give me a hand picking this thing back up."

"I'll help," said Decker stepping forward.

"Me too," said Finch.

The three of them approached the painting. Percy and Finch took hold of the top corners while Decker lifted from the middle. The painting was large and heavy, but when they got it upright, Decker noticed something strange.

"The picture wire isn't broken," he said, gazing at the back of the painting.

"Really?" Percy sounded surprised. "Then how did it come down if the nails are still there?"

"Let's lean it against the wall and see if we can find out," Finch said.

Together, the three of them dragged the painting to the wall, turned it around, and leaned it there with the back facing outward so they could inspect it.

"Mr. Decker is quite correct," Percy said, tugging on the picture wire. "This is just fine."

"Well, paintings don't just leap off the wall of their own accord," Lady Elizabeth said. "Something must've caused it to fall."

"Your guess is as good as mine," Percy said with a shrug. "I'm just glad no one was nearby when it did. The picture frame must weigh eighty pounds. It would give a chap quite a knock on the head."

"Perhaps we should go back to the séance now," Florence said, glancing toward the library. Madame Serafina had risen from the table and now stood in the doorway. "This painting isn't going to help us find Eric."

"Right. Of course." Percy turned to the library.

"Wait," Decker said, looking at the back of the painting. The dust cover, a thin sheet of brown paper, had torn in the top left corner and hung loose. The damage looked fresh and probably occurred when the painting fell to the floor. Behind it, Decker could see the corner of another piece of paper. "There's something behind the painting."

Percy turned back to him. He studied the back of the painting. "Yes. I see it too."

"Then don't just stand there," Lady Elizabeth said. "Let's see what it is."

"You found it. You do the honors," Percy said to Decker. "Tear that paper off."

Decker gripped the torn dust cover and pulled downward. The paper came away easily; the glue used to hold it in place had long ago turned brittle.

Behind it, several more folded sheets of paper, only a little smaller than the canvas itself. They were tucked inside the stretcher bars. They looked old.

"What do you think it is?" Eden asked, inching forward to get a closer look.

"It's probably nothing," said Percy. "Just a bunch of old paper put in there to fill up the space."

"Why would anyone want to do that?" Lady Elizabeth asked.

"I don't know, woman," Percy said, exasperated. "This isn't exactly my area of expertise."

"It's not just paper put in there to fill the gap," Decker said. He lifted the sheets out and went back to the library so that he could lay them on the table.

Madame Serafina stepped aside to let him enter.

"Can we turn the lights up in here?" Decker asked, laying the papers down carefully on top of the black tablecloth.

From out of nowhere, Davies appeared and went around the room, turning up the wall sconces. Decker wondered if he had been lingering nearby, ready to come running.

Everyone else was in the room now. They crowded around the table, eager to see what had been hidden behind the old painting.

Decker unfolded the sheets of paper and laid them out flat. They were brown, their surface foxed with age. It was clear they were old. Perhaps as old as the painting itself.

And something else was clear, too.

Percy gasped as he looked down at them.

Lady Elizabeth shook her head in wonder. "Are those what I think they are?" She asked.

"Yes," Decker said, turning around to face her. "We found the original floor plans for this house."

Thirty-One

"LOOKS like Madame Serafina summoned a ghost after all," Lady Elizabeth said.

"You think that ghost knocked the painting off the wall?" Percy asked, raising an eyebrow.

"Unless you've got a better explanation for this fortuitous timing." Lady Elizabeth looked around the room. "Thank you, Ambrose, wherever you are."

"I think the bigger question is whether there is a priest hole on those plans," Fitzmorris said. "Otherwise, ghost or not, they aren't much use to us."

"I'm looking," said Decker, poring over the unfolded plans. he concentrated on the ground floor, but at first, didn't see anything. The paper was badly discolored, and the plans had been drawn in ink, which had faded and turned brown over the years. It was hard to tell what he was looking at, but soon he identified the grand entrance hall and the surrounding rooms. He traced the lines of the walls with his fingers, unsure what he was supposed to be looking for, until he came to the drawing room. Which was when he noticed a curious feature. The drawing room was not as deep as it should be. The wall ended several feet before the rear wall of the house and the conservatory. A narrow dead space in between was unlabeled.

"I think I've found it," he said, pointing to the gap between the walls. "This is the only anomaly on the plans."

Lord Percy leaned over and examined the spot Decker was pointing to. "By George, I believe you are right."

"Is there a hidden door marked on the map?" Stour asked, straining to see the plans over Decker's shoulder.

"Not that I can tell." Decker wasn't even sure that the mystery space was actually a priest hole, but he couldn't think what else would account for the inconsistency. "They probably didn't mark the door on the plans in case the priest hunters got a hold of them. It would be too obvious."

"I bet those plans have been concealed behind that painting since the house was built," Percy said. "Thank heavens the priest hunters didn't find them, or we wouldn't have discovered the secret chamber."

"Now we have to figure out a way into it," Fitzmorris said. "And we've already examined that wall and found nothing out of the ordinary."

"True." Decker was still studying the plans. "But now we know there must be a hidden door somewhere on that wall." He straightened up and folded the plans. "Let's go find it."

Thirty minutes later, frustrated and no closer to accessing the hidden chamber than they were before, everyone stood looking at the drawing room wall that had so far refused to give up its secrets.

Lord Percy shook his head. "This is a pickle. We know that there is a hidden space behind this wall, but there doesn't appear to be any way to access it. Maybe it isn't a priest hole after all, but just a convenient place to put the plumbing and such."

"This house was built in the sixteenth century," Decker said. "They didn't have internal plumbing and wouldn't have needed anywhere to run pipes."

"Well then, maybe it was just a mistake on the plans."

"I don't think so." Decker nodded toward the drawing room door. "I bet if you measure the internal dimensions of this room, and then measure the length of the wall in the great entrance hall from the point where the drawing room starts to the back of the house, you will find one is longer than the other. There is a hidden space behind this room. I'm sure of it."

"Which doesn't help if we can't get in there," Florence said, sounding desperate. She went to the wall and put her hand against it. "My Eric might be right on the other side of the wall, and we can't reach him."

"There has to be a way in," Decker said. "There aren't any other hidden rooms on the plans, so we must be in the right spot."

"What about behind the fireplace?" Percy said, looking at the leaping flames. "That's the one place we haven't looked."

"It's possible," Decker admitted. "But unlikely. It would be inconvenient if the authorities showed up while the fireplace was in use. You would have to extinguish the fire in order to access the priest hole and then light it again to avoid drawing attention to your subterfuge."

"And all the while, the priest hunters are on your doorstep," Lady Elizabeth said. "Not the smartest place to hide a secret door."

"That doesn't mean they didn't make use of the fireplace," Decker said. A thought had occurred to him. A likely reason why they had not found the mechanism that revealed the hidden door. He went to the fireplace and gingerly reached his hand toward it near the mantle.

The fire had burned down and consumed most of the logs. It was almost out.

The heat was uncomfortable, but not unbearable.

Reaching up into the chimney, he felt around, ignoring the spiderwebs, and something with too many legs that scuttled away at the brush of his fingers.

Then his fingers touched something else behind the mantle. A small metal lever that he thought at first might connect to a damper—a small door above the firebox that could be closed to keep out drafts when the fireplace was not in use—but then he realized this house was too old to have such a device.

Hoping for the best, he pulled on the handle.

The result was instantaneous. With an audible click, one of the wood panels on the right-hand side of the fireplace swung open a couple of inches.

"By Jove, you did it," exclaimed Percy. "Good show, old man."

"We shall see." Decker stepped away from the fireplace. The panel was so well-crafted that when closed, it would have been impossible to see the concealed door. Through the newly revealed gap, he saw nothing but inky blackness. He opened the panel wider to reveal a narrow space running in both directions behind the wall, but it was so dark, he couldn't see more than a few feet in either direction. "Eric?" he called into the murky space. "Are you in there?"

There was no answer.

Florence made a small sound.

Decker called out again, but there was still no response.

He stepped across the threshold into the tight space and turned left, then felt his way along the rough interior walls with his hands, practically blind now. Several feet later, he encountered another wall blocking his way. Turning around, Decker moved in the other direction, passing beyond the open panel and exploring the narrow chamber to the right of the door.

The rest of the group crowded around the opening, watching him.

After going ten or more feet in the darkness, the floor dropped away unexpectedly under Decker's foot. He almost lost his balance and pressed his hands hard against the walls to stop himself from pitching forward. Regaining his balance, Decker probed the void with his foot and discovered a stone step, then another, descending downward under the house.

"There are steps," he called over his shoulder, then backpedaled toward the open panel and stuck his head out, looking at Percy. "This is more than just an old priest hole. Eric isn't here. We're going to need candles to light our way, and quickly."

Thirty-Two

NO SOONER HAD the nightlights shown up, than everyone moved toward the hidden door, eager to venture into the narrow space between the walls and descend into the dark unknown to look for the lost boy. But Decker stopped them. First, he wanted to test a theory. He quickly explained what he wanted to do, stepped back into the darkness, and used a small handle to close the hidden panel behind him.

Decker was now alone in the darkness with only the candle flame for light. He examined the inner skin of the door, including the handle he had used to close it, and came to a startling revelation. There was no way to release the panel from within.

He raised his fist and pounded on the panel.

"Hello. Can you hear me?" he shouted.

There was no response.

Decker was trapped behind the panel just like the boy a hundred years ago, and presumably Eric earlier that day.

But then, after a few moments, there was a click and the

panel opened again. Lord Percy peered at him from the other side. "Find what you're looking for?"

"Yes." Decker stepped back out into the drawing room. "It's impossible to release the panel from the other side. Either there was never a mechanism to do so, or it broke at some point."

"Not surprising. That panel has been there for hundreds of years, and I doubt more than a handful of people have ever used it."

"Could you hear me pounding on the back of the panel and shouting?" Decker asked.

"Yes, but barely. If we weren't standing right next to it and listening, we would never have heard a thing."

"That explains why Ambrose got trapped, and no one ever found him," Eden said. The color had drained from her face. "The poor boy. He must have accidentally found the release for the panel in the chimney and wandered inside to explore."

"The panel closed behind him, and he became trapped," Percy said.

"Not just him." Florence was fighting back tears. "Eric is in there, too."

"Not anywhere close." Her husband replied, peering into the blackness beyond the panel. "Why wasn't he waiting on the other side of the panel?"

"Maybe he couldn't get out and went looking for another means of escape," Decker said. "We need to see what's down those steps."

"What are we waiting for, then?" Lark took moved toward the hidden chamber. "The quicker we get down there, the sooner we'll find him."

"I agree." Florence moved to follow.

Decker raised a hand. "Hold on. There's barely any room in there and we don't know how safe it is. Four of us will go. Everyone else will stay here and wait."

"But—" Florence looked aghast.

"I mean it. We can't afford to have a herd of people tramping around somewhere that has sat unexplored for hundreds of years. Who knows what we'll find?" Decker pointed to Finch and Percy. "The two of you will come with me, along with Edward, because he's the boy's father. Everyone else, just sit tight."

Florence looked like she was going to protest once again, but then thought better of it and closed her mouth.

"Everyone take a nightlight," Decker said, moving toward the hidden panel. "And let's prop this open. I don't want to get trapped on the other side like Ambrose."

Davies was already stepping forward with a heavy chair to prop the panel open.

"Everyone ready?" Decker asked, looking at his small group of explorers.

All three nodded.

"All right. Stay close," said Decker, and then stepped across the threshold into the hidden passageway, with his nightlight raised.

As he moved into the darkness, he heard Finch, Lark, and Lord Percy following behind. He paused and examined the steps, letting the candlelight play over the walls and floor. They were constructed from large blocks of stone slotted together and laid one atop the other.

"Looks safe enough," he said over his shoulder, then lowered a foot tentatively onto the first step.

When it held his weight, he went to the next step, and then the next. Soon, he was at the bottom. Ahead of him, stretching into darkness, was a vaulted tunnel. He moved forward to allow the others to come down while examining his surroundings.

"Huh." Lord Percy drew level with Decker. "I was half expecting to end up in some forgotten corner of the cellar. This must run adjacent to the back wall of the house."

"Where does it go?" Finch asked.

"The only way to find that out is to follow it." Decker started off again, holding the nightlight out ahead of him. There was a cold draft running through the tunnel that caught the flame and made it flicker, forcing him to cup his hand around it to stop the candle from blowing out.

They trudged on in the darkness and soon came to a fork in the tunnel.

Decker stopped. "Left or right?"

"Right," Finch said. "This tunnel can't go on for much longer. We can always double back if we find nothing of interest."

"Or we could split up," Percy suggested.

"No." Decker shook his head. "We don't know how stable these tunnels are, or where they go. I don't want anyone else getting hurt or lost. We stick together."

"Fair enough, old boy."

Decker started off again down the right-hand tunnel. It ran for fifty feet before they reached another set of steps. Unlike the ones at the other end of the tunnel, these were spiral and wound around a central stone column. But there was no way they could climb them. The top half of the column had crumbled, and the steps had collapsed down into the tunnel. It now lay in a heap of broken stone. All they saw above them was a yawning black hole in the ceiling that gave no clue regarding where the steps had once led.

"End of the line, chaps," Finch said.

"I wonder what's up there?" Lark held his candle as high as he could, but the light didn't even make a dent in the darkness above.

"Judging from the direction of our travel, and how far we've gone, I suspect this tunnel runs underground to the chapel," Percy said. "It was probably a way for the priest to escape if he was in the middle of a service when the Queen's soldiers turned up looking for a clergyman to persecute."

"Unless you find the entrance somewhere in the chapel crypt, you may never know for sure," Decker said. "But regardless, Eric isn't in this tunnel, and he certainly didn't climb those steps. We should go back and take the left-hand turn."

They walked back the way they had come and took the other tunnel. This one was longer. At least eighty feet, and it didn't end in a set of steps. Instead, the tunnel opened into an oblong underground room with a vaulted ceiling. Five benches were arranged in the middle of the chamber, facing a narrow stone table at the other end. A crucifix hung at an angle on the rear wall above the table.

"What is this place?" Finch breathed, looking around in awe.

"It's a secret chapel," Percy said, stepping into the room. His footsteps echoed around the walls and up into the ceiling. "The family that owned the manor must have used this to hold secret religious services."

"It was a place to hide the priest from those who wished to kill him, and a place to worship away from prying eyes," Decker said. "Ingenious."

"I had no idea any of this was here." Percy walked around the benches, his fingers trailing over the back of one of them. He approached the stone altar and then stopped, staring down. "You might want to see this."

Decker rushed forward with the others at his heel. When he rounded the altar, he stopped. A small boy was sitting there, curled up. He looked terrified. Next to him was a candle that had burned down to nothing but a pile of melted wax.

Edward Lark let out a cry of relief and dropped to his knees. He took the boy in his hands and held him close. "Eric. I was afraid we would never see you again."

"Um, we aren't alone," Finch said, stepping toward the corner of the room with his candle extended.

Decker followed and raised his own candle. The twin flames illuminated the corner of the hidden chapel in flickering orange light. And the flames illuminated something else, too. A set of bones in ragged clothing leaning against the wall. Bones small enough to be those of a child. They had found Ambrose.

Thirty-Three

HALF AN HOUR LATER, with Eric safely removed from the hidden chambers underneath Blackthorn Manor and being tended to by his parents, the rest of the guests and Lady Elizabeth descended into the tunnels, eager to see the newly discovered secret chapel for themselves. Even Madame Serafina came along, although she looked decidedly uncomfortable, and claimed that she could sense the spirits close at hand, closing in around her.

No one paid her any heed and instead crowded into the chapel where the bones of the boy who disappeared a hundred years ago had laid for a century in the darkness waiting to be discovered.

"I feel so bad for him," Lady Elizabeth said, looking down at the corpse. "To think, his family lived in this house all those years after he disappeared, never knowing that he was so close at hand."

"It's awful," said Eden, clapping her hand to her mouth.

"After Christmas, and when the snow has cleared, we'll bring the constable up here and give this boy a real burial," said Percy.

"There's a private cemetery for the Blackthorn family behind the chapel. We can lay him next to his sisters, Edwina and Jane."

"They'll be together again," Lady Elizabeth said. "You should tell Alistair about this at the earliest opportunity. Ambrose is his ancestor, after all."

"His great, great— something uncle."

"Yes. He'll want to be at the funeral."

"The clothes he's wearing," Daisy said. "They look just like the ones he was wearing when his ghost led me downstairs in the middle of the night."

"Speaking of which, why on earth would Ambrose want to lead Eric off and get him trapped, too?" Percy asked. "The boy could have died. Doesn't seem like a nice thing to do."

Decker had an answer for that. "I don't think he was trying to trap Eric. He was probably happy to find someone who could see him, and he wanted to be found. That's why he suggested playing hide and seek and said he would show Eric somewhere secret."

"A hidey-hole," said Daisy.

"Yes. But Eric got trapped, just like Ambrose had a century earlier. He couldn't get back out the way he came because the latch on the inside of the panel was broken, and he couldn't escape through the chapel because the stairs had collapsed."

"It was an accident, then."

"Yes. Ambrose's ghost must have realized what he'd done and used the energy from the séance to knock the painting off the wall and show us the plans, hoping we would figure it out."

"All's well that ends well," Percy said, turning back toward the tunnel. "I don't know about the rest of you, but I'm exhausted. It's three in the morning and tomorrow is Christmas day. If we don't get some sleep, we'll be no good for the festivities."

"Look." Daisy had turned to follow Lord Percy, but now she was pointing toward the corner of the chapel. "Do you see him?"

"See who?" Eden asked.

"Ambrose." Daisy's eyes filled with tears. "He's standing in the corner of the room, looking at us. I can see him just like I can see the rest of you. He... He looks happy."

"I don't see anything," Decker said, following Daisy's gaze and peering into the corner.

No one else did, either.

Except for Daisy, who walked around the benches and approached the corner, holding out her hand. After a moment, she dropped her arm to her side and looked around with a smile on her face. "He's gone. I think he crossed over."

"He's at peace," Eden said, "because he's finally going to be brought home."

"That's the best Christmas present any of us could hope for." Lord Percy said, before stepping out of the chapel and disappearing into the darkness on his way back to the drawing room.

Thirty-Four

CHRISTMAS MORNING DAWNED bright and clear. The snow had stopped falling and the sky was a dazzling blue. Eric had recovered from his ordeal and appeared to have all but forgotten it in the excitement of opening his presents when they gathered around the tree in the drawing room after lunch.

No one mentioned the events of the previous day. It was like there was an unwritten pact not to spoil Christmas with talk of their harrowing ordeal. Madame Serafina, still unable to return to London because of the blizzard, joined in with the festivities and clung to the hope that she could depart the next day once the groundskeeper, who lived in town, returned to the manor, and cleared the driveway.

In the afternoon, they stood around the piano and sang carols. Afterward, in the down time before Christmas dinner was served, Decker sat near the window in the conservatory and looked out. He was thinking of Nancy, and how far from each other they were, both in distance and time. The book he had purchased as a gift for her two days before—A Christmas Carol —still sat on his shelf back in London. Someday, he hoped she would receive it and know that even stranded over a hundred years in the past, he never stopped thinking of her.

"You look sad," a voice said, breaking through his thoughts.

Decker looked up to see Daisy standing nearby, a worried expression on her face.

"I'm not sad," he said. "Just missing my family."

"Why aren't they here with you?" Daisy settled in the chair opposite him. Between them, on a small table, was the chess game they had played the previous day, the pieces still in checkmate.

"They're a long distance away," Decker replied, feeling a tug at his heart.

"You should cheer up." Daisy started putting the chess pieces back in their original positions. "We are your family today."

"You know, you're right. I should cheer up." Decker pushed the maudlin thoughts from his mind. He had nothing to feel glum about. Not on this day. Things could have been so much worse after he arrived in London. He could have ended up in a workhouse, or stuck in prison as a vagrant, but instead he was surrounded by people who cared about him and enjoying the hospitality of a wonderful couple who had opened their doors to him. Later, they would all gather in the dining room and feast on roast turkey and goose, then warm themselves in front of a roaring fire with a glass of brandy in hand. A century or more in the future, Nancy might be enjoying a Christmas of her own, but he didn't need to feel sad, because for all he knew, there would be a way back and he could enjoy the holidays now, and in the future next to the woman he loved. He could have the best of both worlds. But he wasn't the only one thinking of family that day. Daisy had her own problems.

"Have you discussed the whole seeing ghosts thing with your parents?"

"What do you think?" Daisy looked at him across the chessboard. "I think they are pretending it didn't happen. At least until after the holidays."

"Probably for the best."

"Do you think Ambrose is really at peace?" Daisy asked after a moment's silence.

"You're the one who saw him depart," Decker replied. "What do you think?"

"I think he's happy not to be trapped in that awful priest hole anymore. Father already said I can come home from boarding school to attend the funeral when they have it."

"I'm sure Ambrose will be delighted that you're there," Decker said. "Wherever he is."

"I hope so." Daisy picked up one of the pawns from the chessboard, then put it back down again. "Want to play best out of three?"

"Promise to go easy on me?" Decker replied.

"Not a chance." Daisy grinned. "But I won't tell anyone how badly I beat you."

"When you put it like that, how could I refuse?" Decker said with a laugh. "Let's play."

.

Made in the USA
Las Vegas, NV
18 March 2023

69294052R00090